WHAT TOMORROW
MAY BRING

What Tomorrow May Bring

by

June Davies

Dales Large Print Books
Long Preston, North Yorkshire,
BD23 4ND, England.

British Library Cataloguing in Publication Data.

Davies, June
    What tomorrow may bring.

    A catalogue record of this book is
    available from the British Library

    ISBN   978-1-84262-711-2 pbk

First published in Great Britain in 1994 by
D. C. Thomson & Co. Ltd.

Cover illustration © Rebecca Parkes by arrangement with
Arcangel Images

The moral right of the author has been asserted

Published in Large Print 2009 by arrangement with
June Davies

Dales Large Print is an imprint of Library Magna Books Ltd.

Printed and bound in Great Britain by
T.J. (International) Ltd., Cornwall, PL28 8RW

'She's A Total Stranger!'

'So I won't see you tonight?' Laura Robbins couldn't hide her disappointment as she glanced up into David Hale's face. At 26, he was working hard to establish his market garden. Laura had a part-time job at Monk's Inn in the village, and looked after her younger brother and sister.

'Don't look at me like that!' David protested, reaching across to squeeze her hand. 'Or I'll forget all about the stall and take you off into the country for the day.' It was a tempting prospect.

'Even if it's late, couldn't you still pop in?' Laura began hopefully, carrying the trug of fresh vegetables David had brought through into the cool pantry. 'After I've put Becky to bed, we could have supper together.'

'Best not.' David's voice was regretful. 'I've still got to fix those cold frames. With any luck, I'll have enough glass left over to do that pantry window for you. James has offered to lend a hand, so we should get it done over the weekend. While I'm at it, I'll take a look at the porch roof. Is it still leaking?'

7

Laura nodded bleakly and sighed. 'Spry-glass seems to be falling apart,' she replied, following David into the vestibule of the narrow Victorian house. It was midway along the sea-facing crescent, with tall evergreen hedges and a gnarled apple tree just un-furling new leaves. 'I wanted to have the outside woodwork painted before Dad got home – specially now he's coming ashore for good – but…' Laura opened the heavy front door for him, letting the sharp, salty air come rushing in. 'I just want the house to look nice and clean and comfortable – the way it always did when Mum was alive.'

'Laura! You're doing a terrific job – James and Becky and this house!' David exclaimed. 'Nobody's prouder of you than your father.' He paused in the open doorway, drawing her around to face him. 'Except me…' Tenderly his lips sought hers, but Laura coloured with embarrassment.

She was trying to wriggle out of David's embrace as the garden gate creaked open.

'David! The postie!'

'Let Ted Tattersall find his own girl,' David murmured, insisting upon a final kiss before setting Laura free. As he strode down the uneven path towards his van, he grinned at the postman.

''Morning, Mr Tattersall!' Laura muttered self-consciously.

'Not much today,' the postman commented morosely. 'Bills. A card from the music shop in town – they've got some Beethoven thing James ordered. And a packet for you from your dad. I see he's in Hong Kong again. There before Christmas, too, wasn't he? And before that, Lisbon and Port Said? Sailing the world – that's the life!'

'Mmm, Dad does love the sea,' Laura commented absently, studying the slim Air Mail package. 'But he always says he'd rather stay at home with us. He would have come ashore sooner, if he could have found a decent job.'

'Well, I hope he knows what he's doing.' Ted sniffed doubtfully, starting back down the path. 'I'd hate to take up teaching at his age – even if the pupils are grown men at college!'

Laura couldn't help smiling as she returned to the kitchen. She slit the packet open, and a wallet of photographs slipped on to her lap. And three sealed envelopes.

Becky's name was printed on one in large multi-coloured letters, with a matchstick drawing of Ken racing from his ship towards a fat red pillar-box.

Laura chuckled and quickly opened her own envelope. As usual, Dad began by asking after everyone. Laura … David … James, Becky, Gran and Grandad Jessup. Aunt Helen and Uncle Alex and their children Diane and Ashley.

Laura could practically hear her father's voice… Unfolding the pages, she pictured Ken sitting in his cabin, writing in fits and starts, with all the noise and bustle of the huge cargo ship going on all about him.

But this was quite unlike Dad's usual cheerful, newsy letters.

Have I ever thanked you for all you've done these past six years? He wrote. *When your mum died – even though Gran and Grandad came to live at Spryglass – I saw you grow up all at once. And later, after Grandad's stroke, when they had to move into the flat, it was you who kept our family together, Laura. I don't know what I would have done without you. But I'd do anything for you not to have given up so much.*

'Oh, Dad, you're so wrong!' Laura cried aloud in the empty kitchen. 'I wanted to leave school and help! I love being at home with Becky and James. There isn't anything I'd rather be doing!'

Never a day goes by that I don't miss your mum, Ken's letter went on. *I'll always love her. I want you to know that…*

Coming ashore to start at the college is a huge step for me. It's one thing being a hands-on engineer aboard ship, but a different prospect entirely to be teaching in a classroom. I did have some second thoughts, but now I'm convinced it's the right decision. You'll be able to start living your own life, at last. Maybe even settle down with that young man of yours!

I just don't know how to tell you. I wish I could talk to you face to face! Perhaps it would be easier in the kitchen as we always do when there're things to talk over? You see, I've met someone very special. It was in the little curio shop where I bought that jade dragon for Becky's last birthday. For a long time we were just friends.

Louise is a dressmaker here in Hong Kong. When I got cold feet about accepting the college job, she encouraged me, made me believe in myself and my ability to succeed. So I accepted. I'd started making arrangements to come home when it hit me. After this trip, I'd probably never go back to Hong Kong. Never see Louise again.

I suddenly realised how empty my life would be without her. And then I found Louise felt exactly the same way! We didn't want to be separated – not even for a few weeks. Louise is a lovely woman, Laura. Kind and gentle.

She's bright and clever and she makes me feel I'm alive again…

Laura broke off, feeling a growing alarm. What was Dad trying to tell her? The handful of words on the final page sprang out at her. Laura read them over and over. Disbelieving. It couldn't be true. Just couldn't be.

Laura, love, Ken Robbins concluded simply, *Louise and I have decided to get married.*

11

When James came downstairs a short while later, he expected to see his sister bustling about the kitchen and the table laid and ready for breakfast. Instead, he found Laura sitting, staring into space.

'Laura? Are you all right?' he began, then saw the Air Mail packet and the scattered pages of a letter.

'Is it Dad?' James asked quickly, a note of panic entering his voice. 'Has something happened?'

'No! No, nothing like that,' Laura reassured him at once, gathering up the contents of the packet. 'It is from Dad, but it isn't bad news. At least, I don't think so. What time is it, anyway?'

'It's OK. I'm up early.' James turned as he opened the fridge and poured a glass of orange juice. 'I want to get to school early because there's extra music practice. I can fix my own breakfast.'

'You'll do no such thing!' Laura spread the cloth across the scrubbed square table.

James had matured so much, especially during the last six months. Laura knew he was trying hard to be the man of the family while Dad was away.

'Sit down and drink your juice,' she told him as she finished setting the table. 'Breakfast won't be two ticks.'

'Thanks.' James did as he was told. 'You

didn't wait to open your letter from Dad?'

'Er, no,' Laura answered awkwardly. 'They all came together in the same packet.'

James looked even more surprised as Laura handed over the envelope addressed to him. He made to push it into his school bag. 'I'll save mine for teatime...'

Laura turned from the stove. 'You'd better read it, Jamie.'

Everything James thought, and felt, showed clearly on his face.

Laura watched his expression change as he read.

'Married?' he burst out impulsively, looking across at Laura in consternation. 'I've never thought about Dad getting married again, have you? And to someone we don't even know–' James broke off abruptly. He avoided Laura's eyes, striving to get a grip on his emotions. He couldn't be weak now. He had to be calm for Laura's sake.

Being the eldest, and a girl, she'd been closest to their mother. What must she be feeling now? Now another woman – a stranger – was coming to take Mum's place? Coming to take Laura's place...

'I wonder what she's like?' James pushed a hand through his fair hair.

'Dad sent some photographs!' Laura explained, remembering.

James pounced on the paper wallet, emptying the photographs on to the table. A

Chinese junk crossing Silvermine Bay at sunset, a picturesque island inhabited only by nesting seabirds, a hundred and eight oil lamps burning to celebrate the festival of Star Gods.

'Here!' He snatched up a picture of Ken standing before a sun-washed shrine, a slim, dark-haired woman close to his side.

Brother and sister stared at the photograph. Louise was dressed in a simple cream linen suit. Her face was shadowed by the wide brim of a matching cream hat with pale coffee-coloured flowers trimming the crown.

James threw himself back against the chair in exasperation.

'We can't tell anything from that! Not even what she looks like. Or how old she is.' He indicated Laura's letter. 'Doesn't Dad say anything? How they met? Who she is? Anything?'

'Just that she's a dressmaker in Hong Kong … apparently they've known each other a while,' she added flatly. 'Been friends. Then they realised…' She got to her feet, mechanically serving her brother's breakfast.

'It'll be good for Dad to have someone,' James ventured tentatively. 'And it'll be nice for you. You and David can get married now.'

Laura raised an eyebrow. 'He hasn't asked me!'

'Only because he knows you wouldn't leave us. And there's no room for him here,' James declared stoutly. 'I bet he proposes as soon as he knows you're free to say yes.'

'There's no point in thinking that far ahead,' Laura answered with a smile. 'Now we're over the shock, there's nothing to make a fuss about,' she said sensibly. 'Dad says Louise is a fine woman. She must be nice, or he wouldn't be marrying her. Everything will turn out for the best,' she added optimistically. 'You get off to school now, and have a good day.'

Laura climbed the stairs to the attic bedroom she and Becky shared and pushed open the low door.

'Breakfast in bed!' she called softly. 'It's a special morning!'

'A letter from Daddy!' Becky squealed in delight, seeing the envelope propped against her beaker of milk.

'You don't need to wait until teatime to open it,' Laura perched on the edge of the bed. 'There's some very exciting news inside!'

Becky's eyebrows knitted with intense concentration as she struggled to make out the simple message, stumbling over even the shortest words.

Laura stroked Becky's fair curls, gently prompting and encouraging. Even though her sister didn't remember Mum, Laura was surprised she accepted the news without query.

'If Dad and Louise are married,' Becky commented, scrambling out of her nightie, 'I'll have a mummy like everyone else in my class, won't I?'

'Yes, pet.' Laura swallowed the sudden lump in her throat. 'Why don't you write a letter to Daddy – to Daddy and Louise? We can do it tonight, after school. Now hurry up and get ready.'

While Becky was dressing, Laura picked up the telephone and dialled Riverside Mill. She listened, without surprise, as it rang and rang.

David worked hard and long hours; even so, money was woefully short. The profits from the fruit and veg stall at the midweek street market helped, but Laura was only too aware how desperate the struggle was.

Later, as she shopped in the village, Laura's thoughts were still whirling as the reality of Ken's remarriage – and the many changes it would bring to the family – began to sink in.

'Laura!'

Absently, she glanced around. Then her face broke into a warm smile when she spotted Dan Jessup emerging from the library. Her grandfather limped now, and he was much thinner than before his stroke.

16

When he'd negotiated the final step, he waved his stick triumphantly.

'Couldn't have managed that a few months ago!'

'Grandad!' she reproved gently. 'Behave yourself! You should be taking things easy.'

'You sound just like your gran. Don't fuss,' Dan grieved. 'I'm feeling better than I've done for ages.' He paused. 'You won't mention this to your gran, will you? It'd only upset her. But that flat's driving me mad.'

'I thought you liked it there?' Laura asked in surprise.

The Jessups' ground-floor flat was modern and compact and conveniently situated at the edge of the village.

'It's nice enough,' Dan responded indifferently. 'Grand when I was poorly and couldn't get about. Now...' He shook his head. 'I miss having a garden. Oh, I potter about up at your Auntie Helen's, but it's all coloured chippings and glazed planters. Not a proper garden at all.'

Dan's blue eyes twinkled as he paused for a breather by the pillar-box.

'I was hoping to bump into you,' he confessed. 'I met James on his way to school. He didn't say much but, well, I could tell from his face that something was going on.'

'We've had a letter from Dad.' Laura hesitated, swallowing hard before adding evenly, 'He's getting married. In Hong Kong.'

'He never is! Why, that's grand!' Dan was clearly delighted. 'Good for Ken! Who is she?'

'Her name's Louise,' Laura replied, slightly taken aback. 'We don't know much else about her.'

'I hope they'll be happy,' Dan went on sincerely. 'Ken deserves it. Shall I tell Gran? Or do you want to?'

'I'd like to.'

'Smashing!' Dan nodded enthusiastically. 'Have you time to pop in now? She'll be home.'

Nancy Jessup was having a satisfying day. She liked to keep busy, and thoroughly enjoyed helping to run the cottage hospital shop. Many of the patients were elderly and long stay, and Nancy made a special point of spending time with them. She was thrilled when one of her elderly ladies gave her a thank-you gift that morning.

'Just a little something from my fruit garden, Nancy.' Frail Miss Pendlebury smiled. 'I always do my own bottling, and this was the last batch of blackcurrants before I broke my hip and landed in here! I asked my great-niece to fetch it from my larder.'

Once home in her tiny kitchen, Nancy set to baking. The blackcurrants would make a delicious tart, and Dan would be hungry after his walk.

'I'm home, Nancy!' Dan called. 'And look

18

who I've brought to see you!'

'Laura!' Nancy hurriedly wiped flour from her hands so she could hug her granddaughter. When she heard Laura's news, she could scarcely believe it. 'But Ken's never breathed a word. He's never even said he was considering getting wed again!' She gasped. 'When is he – are they – coming home?'

'They're travelling part of the way on Dad's ship,' Laura explained. 'Then flying the rest. They'll be home by the end of the month.'

'Is she – Louise – from Liverpool?' Nancy asked.

'I'm not sure. Dad didn't say–'

'Is she single?' Nancy went on hurriedly, her mind racing ahead to the possible consequences of Ken's remarriage. 'Or divorced? Or widowed, with children of her own?'

Laura stared at her grandmother blankly. The possibility that Louise might have a family hadn't occurred to her!

'Ken would've said,' Dan said calmly. He saw Nancy was troubled, and wanted to ease her growing anxieties. 'Now, how about a cup of tea? What've you been baking?'

To Laura, the day had seemed endless. Putting the saucepan on to the stove to heat milk for Becky's bedtime drink, she turned wearily to the kitchen table where James was engrossed with his homework.

19

'Why don't you go over to the mill for a bit?' he suggested, glancing up at his sister. She looked worn out. 'It'd do you good to see David.'

Laura couldn't argue with that. 'But aren't you going out?' she queried. 'It's your football night.'

'Even if I wanted to spend three hours training – which I don't – I've half a century of European history to catch up on. You get off. I'll see to Becky's cocoa and read her story.'

'Are you sure?'

'Laura!' he said loudly. 'Go!'

Laura was soon cycling away from the coast towards open fields, where horses and cattle were beginning to settle down for the night. Presently, she heard the burble of the river, which gave David's market garden its name of Riverside. Only the dilapidated slate-roofed mill house still remained, but Grandad had told them how once, long ago, a working flour mill had stood on the bank, drawing its power from the river.

In spite of the gathering gloom, no lights glowed at the mill house's small, square windows. David couldn't be back yet, Laura realised. Had he stopped off in Liverpool for something?

Propping her bike against the hedge, she sat down on the worn stone doorstep to wait. She prided herself on being a calm and capable woman – yet here she was, close to tears in the darkness, longing to rush to the comfort and strength of David's arms like a lost and frightened child.

At last, a heavy vehicle trundled up the rough track and David got down from the cab. 'Laura!' He was delighted to see her. 'What are you doing here at this time of night? I had a flat tyre ... thought I'd never get home.'

As Laura felt the warmth of David's arms encircling her, the last vestiges of control gave way. Clinging to him tightly, she buried her face in his chest and all her bottled-up fears and doubts poured out.

'I want Dad to be happy – of course I do,' Laura concluded, as she sat with David before the crackling open fire in the mill's living-room. 'But, I'm so – so angry at him! He's turned all our lives upside down. How could he do it? Just up and marry a total stranger? How could he?' She met David's eyes miserably. 'I know it's mean and selfish – but I wish he'd never met this woman.'

'It's not mean, or selfish, at all,' David reassured her calmly. 'It's natural. For years, looking after Becky and James and Spryglass has been your whole life. You've been the one to take charge, make decisions. Now you're faced with the prospect of handing it all over. That would be bad enough in normal circumstances, but it's worse for you because you haven't had a chance to get to know Louise.'

'I thought you'd understand,' Laura murmured in disappointment. She'd wanted – needed – David's support. 'You just don't see what this marriage means to James and Becky and me.'

Much later, after he'd taken her home, David worked long into the night patching up some second-hand cold frames. It gave him plenty of time to brood over Laura's cool response to his kisses.

Sleep wouldn't come to Laura the night before her father was due to arrive with his new bride. She lay still, so as not to disturb Becky, but her mind buzzed agitatedly and would allow her no rest. Dawn was lightening up the sky when she finally fell asleep. All too soon Smokey's barking woke her again.

David was down in the garden. He'd brought vegetables and salad, freshly picked that morning. As soon as Laura got back from walking Smokey on the beach, she began washing and peeling. During the wakeful hours of night, she'd made up her mind to be cheerful and composed all day. It had to be a happy occasion for everyone. Nothing must go wrong.

She had the special meal for Dad's homecoming planned down to the final crumb.

Gran and Auntie Helen had wanted to help, but they'd understood when she'd said she wanted to do everything herself. She was making good progress when Becky and James came down to breakfast. They were going to school as usual, but having the afternoon off.

David had offered to drive them all to the airport, but Laura had decided it would be nicer to stay at home and have a special welcome awaiting. Then Dan Jessup had tactfully suggested that only Laura and the children be at Spryglass when the newly-weds arrived.

'Best give them a while to themselves,' Dan had told Nancy and Helen. 'We'll have our chance to say hello when they come to tea on Sunday.'

The hours sped by. Laura was just lifting a large saucepan of vegetables on to the stove, when the front door burst open and Becky came racing into the kitchen, a bulky roll of paper in her hands.

'Wait till you see, Laura!' she cried, dancing up and down excitedly. 'It's called a frieze! I did it in class. Wait till you see – but I'm putting some glitter on first!' Becky was off up to the attic like a whirlwind.

Laura looked at James, who was silently hanging his schoolbag on the peg in the hall. 'I've been dropped from the football team,' he said bleakly. 'The coach said I've missed one too many training sessions.'

'Oh, Jamie!' Laura exclaimed. 'That's bad luck!'

'I don't mind – not about the football, at least,' James went on honestly, coming into the kitchen. 'It'll give me more time for my music – and revising.' His A-levels were just around the corner. 'It's Dad I mind about. He'll be so disappointed.'

'No, he won't. He'll be so glad to be home. Would you like me to tell him?'

James shook his head. 'No, I'll do it.' He hesitated. 'Would it be cowardly to leave it till tomorrow?'

'I think it'd be tactful. And considerate,' Laura reassured. 'Give him – them – today to get settled. There'll be lots of time for talking later.'

While Laura got on with melting the chocolate for topping the celebration cake, James wandered thoughtfully into the dining-room. Whenever he was troubled, James sought refuge in music. He began playing softly on the second-hand upright piano his mother had got for him when he was eight years old. Mum had always understood and encouraged him... James's fingers moved lightly over the yellowed keys. It was going to feel strange, having another woman in the house.

Becky clattered down the stairs with the

unrolled frieze draped over her open arms. 'I've finished it, Laura!' she called, hurtling into the kitchen. 'I've put the glitter on! It's for Louise and Dad's room! Look, I've drawn Smokey and–' she stretched her arms out even farther.

'Be careful!' Laura's cry of warning came too late. The plastic bowl toppled from the table, and the melted chocolate oozed out over the floor.

'Thank goodness it wasn't hot!' Laura gasped in relief, kneeling to wipe splashes from Becky's bare legs.

Leaving Becky putting up the colourful frieze in Ken and Louise's room, Laura hurried into the dining-room, where James was scribbling notes on to the back of an envelope.

'Will you go to the village and buy more chocolate? Becky's just spilled all we had.'

'Sure.' James got up at once. 'No problem.' On his way out to the back garden for his bike, he passed by the cooker. He glanced round at Laura. 'Shouldn't the stove be hot? None of these pans are.'

When David Hale arrived a short while later, he found Laura crouching in the cramped cupboard under the stairs, a torch gripped between clenched teeth. She felt hot and dusty and frustrated and on the verge of panic. In less than two hours, Dad and Louise would be here. And half of the meal was still standing uncooked on a cold stove!

'Hi, there!' David's face broke into its easy smile. 'You look like you're having fun! Not only pretty, but a competent electrician, too.'

'Don't mention electricity to me!' Laura warned, backing out of the cupboard. 'Not a word, David!'

'Fine by me.' He grinned. 'I'd much rather kiss you–'

'Fool!' She struggled free, smiling at him as they went through to the kitchen.

'I came to see if you needed an extra pair of hands.' David stopped at the puddle of chocolate and the upturned bowl in the middle of the floor. 'But I see everything's under control.'

'If you really want to help, you could clear that lot up!'

'Right away, ma'am,' he replied, getting down on his knees with a wet cloth. 'I know my place.'

Laura went to the dresser and carefully took out the best crockery.

'Your cake looks fantastic, Becky!' David exclaimed admiringly, as the little girl put the finishing touches to the thick, chocolatey topping. 'Can I scrape out the bowl?'

'You shouldn't really,' Becky replied severely. 'But you can – because I've got to go and put my new dress on.' She pushed the bowl into David's arms and hurried upstairs.

Laura had already changed into a full-skirted, primrose dress. As she moved about the dining-room, fussing with the table and the flowers, David couldn't keep his eyes from her. It was wonderful to see her back to her old self, laughing and smiling, her blue eyes dancing. David had no way of knowing it was simply the result of tension and anxiety.

Following her into the kitchen, he slipped his arms about her waist, kissing the nape of her neck. Her skin was soft, her hair scented.

'Marry me, Laura…' David breathed impulsively. 'Marry me now!'

'Don't be ridiculous!' Laura blazed, her frayed nerves finally snapping as she spun round. 'How can I possibly marry you?'

'But you – you're free now,' he began in confusion, reaching for her again.

Laura pushed away from him. 'If I couldn't leave Becky before, how can I leave her now? Louise may be my father's wife, but she certainly isn't Becky's mother! She's a total stranger. Do you really expect me to trust Becky…?'

'Laura! Laura!' Becky burst into the room. 'They're here! They're here!'

With Becky and Smokey racing on ahead to the gate, Laura, David and James gradually spilled out from the house on to the stone steps. They were staring down the garden path as a taxi was pulling to a halt.

His face creased in a broad smile, Ken Robbins stepped from the taxi. He waved and called greetings, then swung Becky up into his arms and hugged her. When he'd put her down, he helped his new wife out of the cab.

'Like It Or Not...'

'Louise,' Ken Robbins was saying proudly. 'These are my children. Becky and James ... and Laura...'

Laura's rehearsed words of welcome dried in her throat. The petite, fashionable woman standing before her was nothing like she'd imagined.

'Hello, Laura.' Louise smiled.

Laura returned the greeting mechanically. She was quite unable to take her eyes from the face of this delicately-beautiful Eurasian girl, only a few years older than she was. She stared with disbelief into the dark eyes of the lovely young girl who was her father's second wife.

As the newcomer smiled hesitantly, Laura floundered for something to say to break the embarrassed silence.

'Shall – shall we go indoors?' she faltered at last, ushering Louise ahead of her up the path. 'I daresay you'd like to freshen up. Dinner will be ready whenever you and – and Dad – are.'

The family crowded into the hall, and suddenly everyone was talking at once. The old house was filled with noise and voices and Smokey's excited barking.

David was bringing in the last of the luggage when Ken Robbins clapped him on the shoulder.

'Your turn next, is it?' Ken inquired cheerfully, oblivious to Laura's horrified glance. 'I expected to come home to find the pair of you engaged at the very least!'

'Dad!' Laura muttered with acute embarrassment, her face flaming.

'Oh, all right, Becky!' Ken good-naturedly turned away as his younger daughter tugged on his hand. 'Let's have a look at this picture of yours!'

'Sorry about that.' Laura couldn't meet David's eyes. 'I'm sure Dad didn't mean...'

'I know. He thinks you're in love with me,' David returned crisply, staring out into the vestibule. 'I made the same mistake myself!'

'David!' She ran after him, catching hold of his sleeve. 'Don't go!'

David looked down at her, stony-faced.

'I can't cope with this alone,' Laura pleaded. 'Stay for dinner. Please?'

'So, after graduating from college, I started out as a dressmaker and designer,' Louise explained as they ate. 'I commenced business on the eighteenth day of the first moon, in the hope that the star gods would bestow prosperity, wealth, joy and longevity upon my little shop–' She laughed, her dark eyes shining. 'But in the beginning, I *still* had terribly hard times!'

'I know all about that!' David chipped in amiably. 'Is there a lucky deity for struggling market gardeners?'

'I'm sure there is,' Louise replied with a brilliant smile. 'There seems to be one for almost everything.'

Yet another, rather awkward, lull descended. The mood in Spryglass's flower-filled dining-room was uneasy, and Laura was inwardly willing the meal to be quickly over. The celebration dinner she had so carefully planned tasted like dust in her mouth. And she was worried about David. He'd agreed to stay, but there had been no trace of his former affection. He'd seemed so cold and distant ... to her at least. He was certainly managing to chat to Louise easily enough.

Becky was too shy to speak to Louise, but sat beside her hanging on her every word, her eyes never leaving her stepmother's face.

Presently, Laura brought in the splendid cake, with its sumptuous chocolate frosting, clusters of sugar flowers and glimmering candles.

Louise turned to Becky and asked about the painting the little girl had hung in her and Ken's room.

Laura frowned. Louise might be making an effort to draw Becky out, but she spoke to her as though she were another adult, instead of a small child longing for a mother.

Laura returned to her place between James and David, experiencing a prickle of resentment.

Only a handful of years might separate them, but she hadn't a thing in common with this poised, worldly-wise young woman.

'Louise ran a very successful business in Hong Kong,' Ken told her. 'She gave it all up to marry me.'

'Darling, you exaggerate!' Louise had overheard. 'My shop was hardly haute couture!' she protested, leaning over to kiss his cheek.

'Is your family in Hong Kong?' James asked politely.

'My father is in Hong Kong. He has an antiques' business there,' Louise replied. 'My mother's a fashion journalist. After they divorced, she returned to France, while I stayed with Father in Hong Kong.'

She sipped at her glass and smiled at him.

'I understand you enjoy music?'

James' face brightened for the first time.

'Oh yes, I'm in the school orchestra. And I compose a bit—' He broke off, darting a quick look to Ken, hoping that the subject wouldn't turn to football. But it did.

'Music's OK for a hobby,' Ken remarked. 'But professional football could be a real career. Jimmy has natural ability – and real prospects – the team coach told me. You're going to play for England one day,' he concluded with a proud smile. 'Aren't you, son?'

It wasn't exactly a question, so James lowered his eyes and said nothing.

Laura knew exactly how he must be feeling and gave him a sympathetic kick under the table. How on earth was he going to tell his father he'd been dropped from the team?

Laura was grateful to escape to the solitude of the kitchen. She was startled by the touch of a cool hand on her bare arm.

'Laura, that was a wonderful meal.' She hadn't heard Louise following her. 'Thank you so much for going to all this trouble,' Louise went on with a smile. 'May I help with the washing up?'

'Certainly not! You're our guest – guest of honour,' Laura corrected herself quickly. 'Do go back to the others.'

Louise smiled again, but this time it did not reach her eyes. She started back across the kitchen as David appeared in the doorway. He gave her a warm smile and held the door open for her.

'Are you going to chase me away, too?' he asked, taking off his jacket and rolling up his shirt sleeves. 'A bit sharp just now, weren't you? It was nice of Louise to want to help.'

'If I was rude, I'll apologise,' Laura returned crisply.

'I understand this is a difficult situation for you,' David ventured carefully. 'But it can't be easy for Louise, either.'

Laura threw a scathing glare at him.

'I suppose you're going to tell me she's the ideal wife for my father?'

'Why wouldn't she be?' David shrugged, joining her at the sink. 'Louise is a kind, intelligent woman. I like her.'

'You've made that perfectly obvious!'

'Laura ... this just isn't like you!' David said in exasperation. 'Can't you even try to see things from Louise's point of view? She's a stranger coming to a strange country, suddenly part of a close-knit–'

'For heaven's sake, David!' Laura cried in despair, spinning round to confront him. 'She's twenty-six years old. Dad's nearly forty-eight!'

'The age difference isn't bothering them – so it has no business bothering anybody else,' David replied shortly, his patience wearing thin.

'It's easy to see whose side you're on!'

'There's no question of taking sides,' David retorted tersely. 'Ken and Louise are married. Like it or not, you'll have to accept it!'

'Well, that's certainly put me in my place, hasn't it?' she snapped, hot colour in her pale cheeks.

'Laura, be reasonable! I'm only saying–'

David broke off abruptly and snatched his jacket from where he'd left it over the chairback. 'Oh, what's the point!'

Laura swung around, swallowing hard to control the tremor in her voice.

'Where are you going?'

'Home,' he said over his shoulder, as he opened the kitchen door. 'Don't you realise I didn't want to argue about Ken and Louise? I wanted to talk to you about us! But it seems there's no point in that, either!'

When the over-excited Becky had finally fallen asleep, and James had disappeared into his room to finish his homework, the conversation between Laura and the newly-weds gradually faded to quietness. The couple were sitting together, Ken's arm round Louise's shoulders, her head on his chest.

Laura grew more and more uncomfortable.

'Anyone for a last cup of tea?' she ventured at last, already on her feet.

'Oh, no, thank you,' Louise murmured, opening drowsy eyes. 'Ken?'

'Not for me. I'm ready to turn in.' He smiled tenderly at his wife. 'Coming, love?'

She nodded, returning his smile and reaching up to kiss his cheek.

Laura looked away quickly, unable to conceal her embarrassment.

After they'd gone upstairs, she went

around tidying up, as she did last thing every evening. Somehow, the homely rooms didn't seem quite like home any more.

It had been a long, long day, but Laura was convinced she wouldn't sleep. Eventually she started up to the attic bedroom she and Becky shared. Then when she reached the shadowy stairwell, she froze...

Ken and Louise were tiptoeing from the room, closing the door carefully behind them. Tears filled Laura's eyes ... she felt excluded ... shut out...

The couple paused on the landing. Ken's hands slipped about Louise's waist, his lips touching hers in a lingering kiss.

Anger flared now. How could Dad have married someone so unsuitable? Yet even as the thought passed through Laura's mind, she found herself longing for the closeness the newly-weds were sharing.

Why had she let David walk out? No – why had she driven him out?

Laura ached with loneliness.

Although Louise's apartment in the peak district of Hong Kong offered panoramic views of the city and the harbour where traditional sampans jostled for space with modern shipping, she'd rarely given the ocean a thought. Her first impression of Spryglass was that wherever she was in the narrow old house it was impossible to ignore the sea's nearness.

The persistent sound of surging waves was always there, and the sharp, cold smell of it.

Louise thought she could even taste salt on her lips as she paused on the sand-dusted garden path, with its borders of early primroses, and waited for Ken to join her. He was going to show her round Sandford, then they were going on to the local bank.

Finally, they'd pop in to say hello to Ken's parents-in-law, Dan and Nancy Jessup.

Louise turned as Ken came down the steps and joined her.

'You look great, love!' he said, brushing her cheek with a quick kiss and slipping his arm around her shoulders.

Louise squeezed his arm, glad to be completely alone with him again, even if it was only for a short while. Amidst so much that was unfamiliar, she had needed Ken's reassurance. It was wonderful to see him looking at her like this ... as he'd done when they exchanged their marriage vows...

'It's a bit misty this morning,' Ken remarked as they started through the garden gate, glancing over the miles of sea and shore. 'But you can just make out the Welsh hills across the water there.'

Louise nodded, scanning the grey ocean and the beach with its flocks of seagulls.

'I don't remember ever seeing so much empty space before!' she exclaimed, comparing it with Hong Kong's brilliant, bustling streets and constant vitality. Here, there wasn't a building for as far as the eye could see. Or another person besides herself and Ken.

'Or hearing so much silence!' she added with a laugh.

'That's because you're a city girl, Mrs Robbins!' Ken grinned back at her, as they turned away from the coast and started towards the village. 'Even in the dead of night, the sea and shore are never completely silent. There's always some sound. Wait until you get used to it, then you'll know what I mean!'

The lane was broad, lined with hedges, old fences and gnarled trees whose branches met overhead in great, green arches.

A boy on a placid-looking bay mare trotted from the deep shadows of the pine wood. He walked past the couple before cantering for the beach.

'Are there stables nearby?' Louise asked.

'Mmm, the other side of the woods. Near the river,' Ken answered. 'Not far from David's market garden. Can you ride?'

'I used to. But I haven't done much since I was young.'

'As long ago as that, eh?' Ken sounded good humoured, but Louise saw his expression become serious. She guessed his joke had sparked a sharp reminder of their homecoming. He hadn't said a word to her about it, but she had sensed his dismay at his children's reaction.

'They were surprised, that's all,' Louise whispered, reaching up to kiss him. 'Just give them time, darling!'

'Yes,' he said with a confidence he hardly felt. 'You're right.' At least, he hoped she was right. He'd realised – too late – that he should have told the children everything about Louise.

Laura, in particular, needed to know how he felt about her.

Instead, he'd shied away from the subject and avoided mentioning how much younger she was. He hadn't wanted them to get the wrong idea. He'd been convinced that, once they'd met Louise, got to know her, they'd understand. For weeks, he'd looked forward to bringing the woman he loved home to his family.

'Is Sandford like the place you grew up in Scotland?' Louise interrupted his thoughts as the old sandstone church came into view.

Ken shook his head, looking at the clusters of stone cottages, small-windowed, some thatched, and the low, bow-fronted village shops.

'I was born in a pit town. Coal-mining, that is,' he explained. 'It was just after the war and the pit was on its last legs. My older brothers were laid off, my father was on short time.' Ken shrugged dismissively; he'd never found talking about himself easy. 'The mine was the town. There wasn't anything else. My sister and I went to relatives in the Highlands until I left school at fifteen. Not much education. No prospects. No hope of a job.

'An uncle of ours lived near Liverpool. He had a scrapyard – and three daughters!' Ken grinned slightly. 'He knew how my family was fixed, and he wrote saying he needed two strong lads to work in his yard. That's how my brother and I ended up in Liverpool.'

'It must have been difficult for you,' Louise murmured.

'I suppose it does seem a bit grim, looking back,' he admitted. 'At the time, it was all right. There were plenty worse off. Ewan couldn't wait to go back north but I'd seen the sea and I knew that was the only life I wanted. So, as you know, I studied at night school and got a job with the shipping line,' he concluded with a smile. 'And I've been at sea ever since!'

'Until now.'

'Until now,' he repeated quietly.

'Any regrets, Ken?' she asked, searching his face earnestly.

'Not a one,' he answered firmly, raising her hand to his lips. 'But staying ashore is going to take some getting used to,' he admitted ruefully. 'I've never really lived here. Sandford was Jeanette's home. I have to keep reminding myself that I won't be sailing away any more. I'm here for good. It's an odd feeling.' He shrugged sheepishly. 'So is starting a new job at my age!'

'The college is fortunate to get you!'

'I wish I had your confidence in me! I've spent nearly thirty years working as an engineer. I'm just not sure how I'll cope with teaching people to be engineers.'

'Darling,' Louise began seriously. 'You'll be–'

'Wonderful – I know!' He grinned as they strolled past the newsagent's, and crossed the curving, tree-lined road to where the bank was sandwiched between the post office and the chemist. 'Sure you don't want to come into Liverpool with me later?' he asked. He was going to collect various documents from his former employers.

'I'd only be in the way,' Louise replied, casting a backward glance at the picturesque village as Ken held the door of the bank open for her to enter. 'Besides, I'd like to explore a little more.'

When Ken had proposed that warm evening on board a sampan in the sun-streaked bay, Louise had accepted without hesitation, even though she knew she'd have to give up everything familiar. Family, friends, home and career would all be left far behind as she travelled half the world to begin life as Ken's wife.

He'd spoken about his children often, showing Louise their photograph and sharing their letters with her. But, still, Laura James and Becky had remained remote, distant figures.

Louise had been too excited and too blissfully happy, to worry about meeting the Robbins children for the first time. In fact, she hadn't given it a thought until the moment she'd stepped from the taxi and met Laura's cool gaze. There had been no friendliness in her stepdaughter's stiffly-polite greeting – only shock and suspicion. And it had unnerved Louise.

She'd tried to hide her feelings, hoping no-one – especially Ken – would guess her discomfort. But now, walking at Ken's side across the village green, Louise admitted she was concerned at the prospect of meeting the parents of Ken's late wife.

'I hope they like me,' she murmured.

'They will. And you'll like them!' Ken replied confidently, tightening his grip on her hand encouragingly. 'Dan and Nancy have been like parents to me. My own died when I was nineteen and I've lost touch with my brothers and sister.'

Louise knew Ken was only trying to re-assure her, but his words only increased the pressure. She was more desperate than ever to be liked and accepted. She took a deep breath as Ken rang the doorbell of the modern ground-floor flat. The tidy window boxes were filled to overflowing with velvety pansies. The door opened, and the genuine warmth of the elderly couple's smiles instantly set her at ease.

'Come in!' Dan Jessup was beaming. 'Let's get a look at the newly-weds!'

Ken made the quite unnecessary introductions, and Dan gently clasped Louise's hand in both of his own.

'It's grand to see you, Louise,' he said sincerely. 'I hope you and Ken have every happiness.'

'Oh, thank you so much!' Louise exclaimed softly, uncharacteristic tears not far from her eyes. 'You're very kind.'

Nancy Jessup was hugging Ken. She hesitated only a moment before giving Louise a hug.

'Welcome to the family!' Nancy's face broke into an even broader smile as she drew Louise into the neat living-room. 'Sit down and make yourself at home,' she instructed, bustling through to the kitchen. 'I'll just put the kettle on.'

'I see you've done a bit of shopping,' Dan remarked as he carefully set the tray with the blue willow-patterned cups and saucers on the coffee table. 'At Almond's, eh?' he went on, eyeing the brown and white striped paper bag at Louise's side. 'Met Hilda Almond did you?'

Louise heard Ken's muffled chuckle, and nodded, looking rather shamefaced. 'Don't remind me!' she replied, taking her purchase from the paper bag to show Dan and Nancy. 'I'd left Ken at the bank, and I spotted this instant camera in the window of the chemist's. It seemed such a good idea to buy it, so I can enclose some photographs when I write to my father. I went inside and asked for the camera–' Louise raised her eyebrows. 'That's when I realised I hadn't any English money!'

'You had a lucky escape there!' Dan exclaimed with a straight face. 'It's a wonder Hilda Almond didn't call the police and have you arrested!'

'Take no notice – Dan's just pulling your leg!' Nancy chipped in, seeing that Louise wasn't quite sure how to take Dan's sense of humour. 'Hilda's all right. We were at school together. She's just–' she searched for the right word '–efficient!'

'She's terrifying,' Dan contradicted flatly. 'Ever since I accidentally dropped a bottle of cough medicine, I haven't dared set foot in the shop! I have to ask Nancy to get my razor blades!'

Dan was laughing now, and Louise and

the others joined in.

'I felt such a fool with my handful of worthless Hong Kong dollars!' Louise admitted. 'And guilty – Mrs Almond was very disapproving! Anyhow, Ken came to my rescue and I got my camera. After I've taken my pictures, perhaps Becky would like the camera? She might enjoy taking photographs and seeing them appear straight away.'

'Oh, that's a nice idea!' Nancy smiled. 'I'm sure she'll be thrilled. She's been so excited, waiting for you and Ken to get home. How are the bairns?' she added, refilling Ken's teacup.

'I wish I knew!' Ken gave a perplexed sigh. 'Laura and David … Jimmy … even Becky. I can't open my mouth without putting my foot in it! Nothing's as I expected it to be.' He looked from Nancy to Dan's concerned face. 'I feel like a stranger to my own family.'

'Time'll put that right,' Nancy replied reassuringly. 'You've been away the best part of six months, Ken. The children are growing up fast. They're changing and so are their lives.'

'Nancy's right,' Dan agreed. 'It's like during the war. When I came home from the Army, I was different and so was everybody else. We all had to get to know each other again.'

'Just take it slowly,' Nancy finished with a smile. 'It'll all work out – then you'll wonder what you were fretting about!'

'My wife's given me much the same advice!' Ken remarked, returning Nancy's smile and helping himself to another piece of her parkin. 'Thanks. No-one can touch your baking, Nancy! By the way, how are Helen and the family? I tried to ring her earlier, but got no reply.' He turned to Louise. 'Helen is Dan and Nancy's younger daughter. She and her family moved away from Sandford last year.'

'Ay, Sandford wasn't good enough for Alex – Helen's husband,' Dan commented with feeling. 'He always was uppity.'

'Dan!' Nancy reproached with a frown.

'Well, it's true! They moved to a new bungalow out at Ingle Green. We don't see as much of Helen and the children as we used to. You'll meet Helen – and Ashley and Diane – on Sunday when they come to Spryglass for tea. Alex, too,' Dan finished, chewing on the stem of the pipe he wasn't allowed to smoke since his stroke. 'If he can spare the time to come, that is!'

Louise and Ken parted in the village. When he hurried off to catch the Liverpool train she wandered round the village. She looked, with interest, into Sandford's one and only dress shop, bought some air mail stationery from the newsagent's and chose a pretty potted plant as a thank-you present for Dan and Nancy.

Despite telling Ken she could find her way back to Spryglass without any trouble, Louise took a wrong turning somewhere near the church. When she finally arrived back at the old house, fine needles of cold rain were dashing from the brooding grey sky.

Grateful for the warmth of the kitchen, Louise peeled off her lightweight jacket. Her fabric shoes were wet through and stained with mud and grass and she kicked them off, too. Shivering, she switched on the kettle for coffee and hurried upstairs to change. She really would have to do some shopping for warmer clothes – and a few pairs of sensible shoes.

When she came down again and had made her hot drink, it was so dark she had to turn on the lights. An off-shore wind was blowing and draughts stirred the curtains around the windows and whistled under the door.

Cupping the coffee mug in her cold hands, Louise peered out through the window to the dripping, windswept garden. A storm was brewing. James and Becky would be cold and wet when they got home from school. And Laura from the hotel…

She went through to the pantry, thinking about cooking the evening meal. But she didn't know much about cookery. What could she make? She didn't even know what her new family liked to eat. Her eyes slid along the well-stocked shelves, then she noticed a jug of sauce and several covered bowls. Evidently, Laura had supper already planned. Even to the carefully-selected potatoes...

Laura Misses David

Louise hadn't been alone in Spryglass before. In the quietness of the rainy afternoon, she wandered inquisitively through the rooms. There was so much of Ken's late wife still present. The furnishings and colour schemes ... the books and ornaments, were obviously Jeanette's choice.

Absently taking the pile of Becky's freshly pressed school clothes from the ironing board, Louise went upstairs to the girls' attic bedroom.

What sort of woman was Jeanette Robbins? Had she and Ken been happily married? Louise was frankly curious. She didn't even know what Jeanette had looked like. That question was unexpectedly answered as Louise was putting Becky's clothes into the top drawer of the tallboy. There, tucked carefully amongst the blouses and nighties, was a framed photograph of Jeanette and Ken on their wedding day.

'What are you doing with that?'

Louise started violently. The photograph slipped from her hands to the hard wooden floor.

'Laura! Oh, I'm so sorry!' Louise bent to

retrieve the jagged pieces of glass from the broken picture frame, but Laura pushed her aside.

'Leave it. Just leave it alone!' She was fighting back tears.

'I didn't mean to pry,' Louise tried to explain. 'It was just in the drawer and—'

'This was Mum's favourite photo.' Laura was furious she was so distressed. 'Grandad made the frame. Now it's ruined!'

'Perhaps it can be repaired?' Louise suggested desperately.

'Don't touch it!' Laura snatched the photograph out of Louise's reach. 'Haven't you done enough? Do you know why Becky hid Mum's picture like that? It was so you wouldn't see it and feel hurt!'

'But I don't want to take her mother's place, Laura!'

'You couldn't!' Laura returned passionately, her emotions finally boiling to the surface. 'You could never take Mum's place!'

The old clock on the mantelpiece noisily ticked away the long, tense seconds as the two women stared at each other in silence. Then Laura dropped to her knees. Hands trembling, she began to pick up the fragments of glass from the smashed picture frame.

Mum had never enjoyed having her photograph taken. There were so few pictures to remember her by… This one, of her and Dad on their wedding day, was cherished. Laura picked up a scarf and carefully wrapped it round the photograph and broken frame.

'You don't belong here!' she blurted out, holding the bundle close to her. Even as she spoke, Laura realised she was being malicious. But she still couldn't halt the torrent of bitter, hurtful words. 'All Mum wanted was Dad – and us – and her home. But that'll never be enough for you, will it? Since the day you arrived, you've done nothing but talk about Hong Kong and your shop and your career and your ambitions. You don't want to be a wife and mother! I don't know why you married Dad at all!'

Louise drew back in shock. She'd never even suspected the truth depths of Laura's resentment. But there was pain there, too, raw and exposed. Louise's anger evaporated. She wanted only to comfort the unhappy girl before her, who suddenly looked so young and vulnerable.

'You and I – we have more in common than you know,' she began gently. 'I know what it's like to lose a mother.'

'How can you say that?' Laura demanded incredulously. 'You don't know what it's like. You can't! Your mother is still alive!'

'That's true, but she left when I was little,' Louise replied slowly. 'I grew up without her. Will you tell me about your mother, Laura?' Louise asked tentatively, perching on the corner of the bed. 'I'd like to know about her.'

Laura turned away, her whole body rigid. She opened a drawer and put away the scarf-wrapped frame. 'You may be my father's wife – and Spryglass is your house now.' Her voice was unusually brittle. 'But this is still my room – mine and Becky's–' Tears began spilling from Laura's eyes, and she kept her back to Louise so they would not be seen. 'Please go away and leave me alone!'

Louise went downstairs to the kitchen, and started unpacking the things she'd bought after she'd left Ken in the village. Finally, when only the brown and white striped paper bag containing the instant camera remained, she paused. Would it be such a good idea, passing it on to Becky, after she'd taken some photographs to send to her own father in Hong Kong?

Ken and Nancy and Dan Jessup had obviously thought so. But what about Laura? Perhaps she might not approve of her giving the child an expensive present?

Ken had brought presents from Hong Kong for all the family, but he hadn't handed them out yet. He wanted to wait until Dan and Nancy came to tea on Sunday and give them theirs at the same time. Perhaps it would be wisest if the camera was just quietly slipped in among Becky's other presents?

Louise frowned. She wanted to be friends with Laura – but her stepdaughter didn't even seem willing to meet her halfway! She tried to imagine how she would have felt if her father had brought home a wife, but the comparison was quite impossible. For much of the time, Louise had been cared for by their housekeeper. She'd had her father's love, and everything his money could buy, but she'd been deprived of his company. Sometimes she'd felt very lonely indeed.

She sighed, staring through the kitchen window. Rain was streaming down, gushing from the gutters and gurgling into the rainwater butt outside the back door.

Louise absently turned her wedding band round her slim finger. She was accustomed to confronting and resolving problems, to dealing with employees and customers and business contacts... But nothing had prepared her for coping with what was facing her now!

Louise switched the kettle on for tea and got out two cups and saucers. She and Laura had to talk. Alone, and now.

Before the rest of the family came home. She heard Laura's footsteps coming down the stairs. She came quietly into the kitchen, her eyes red rimmed, her cheeks pale.

'I'm making tea,' Louise said uneasily.

'Would you like a cup?'

Laura nodded hesitantly and pulled back one of the pine chairs and sat down at the table. 'Thank you.'

Louise poured Laura's tea and added milk. Then a slice of fresh lemon to her own cup. 'Laura,' she began deliberately. 'You and I have to—'

Laura rose from the table abruptly, her tea untouched. 'James and Becky will be home shortly.' She crossed to the sink, her trainers noiseless on the stone-flagged floor. 'I'll have to start supper.'

Louise watched Laura wash her hands, then tie on a clean apron before going into the pantry. 'I've peeled the potatoes,' she said, following.

Laura's mouth tightened.

'Wasn't that right?' Louise asked.

'I'd planned to bake them.' Laura forced a smile. 'Jacket potatoes are Dad's favourite. I'd already done the ingredients for the filling. Now I'll have to make something else.'

'I'll help you.'

Laura tensed. No doubt Louise meant well, but she'd be more of a hindrance than help. She had her own ways of doing things and would get on much quicker by herself. The children and Dad would be cold and wet when they came home. She wanted a hot meal ready and waiting for them.

'There's no need for that, Louise.'

'I think there is!' Louise tried to keep her voice even. She was unsure exactly how to broach the subject, but determined to say what needed to be said. 'I'm not a guest, you know. Besides, it's not fair for you to do all the work. You have your job—'

'I don't mind. I'm used to it. And I love cooking,' Laura replied, bustling past her. 'After you're settled in, we'll see.'

'I am settled in.' Louise struggled to be tactful, to keep her voice friendly and casual, as though this conversation wasn't of the utmost importance. 'I admit I've never run a house, or been responsible for a family, or a child... And I don't want to push you out. But I'm Ken's wife now. This is my home. My family. I think it's time I started caring for them.' She braced herself for Laura's response, half-expecting another outburst. None came.

Laura was grating the peeled potatoes into a bowl. She didn't look up, didn't attempt a reply, because she knew her voice would betray her. She'd been desperately trying to cling to something which was gone for ever. Being angry and resentful was no use. It wouldn't change anything. Louise's unruffled tone, her calm, reasonable words echoed in Laura's mind. She was Dad's wife. Spryglass was hers, now. Everything was hers. And Laura could do nothing but accept it.

She got on with the meal.

Louise fussed about the kitchen behind her, taking dishes from the dresser, setting the table, placing the bowl of fresh flowers in the centre.

Smokey's sudden ear-splitting bark startled them both.

The little dog rushed in from the dining-room, where he'd been watching out of the window. He raced through the kitchen, claws clattering, barking wildly, and began scratching at the back door. James and Becky, followed by Ken, burst into the warm, welcoming kitchen.

'Here we are, home from the sea!' Ken grinned, dripping rainwater as he kissed Louise's cheek. 'Or at least, home from school and town!'

'Daddy waited for us at the corner.' Becky laughed, kneeling to fuss her ecstatic dog. 'He raced us home!'

'Is this all the post?' James asked, hardly out of his drenched school coat before going to the dresser to check the envelopes propped behind the Toby jug. 'Wasn't there anything for me, Laura?'

'Waiting for a billet-doux from Charlotte, are you, Jimmy?' Ken winked broadly at Louise. 'He's got a pretty wee lassie keen on him!'

'Charlotte and I are friends, Dad,' James

returned with amiable patience. 'Just friends. And we sit next to each other in school – so she doesn't need to send me letters!'

Laura was disentangling Becky from Smokey, and unfastening the little girl's soaked coat. 'You're wet right through!' She gave Becky a quick cuddle before hurrying her towards the stairs. 'We'll get you dried off, then I'll make hot chocolate–'

'I'll make the drinks, Laura.' Louise was already gathering mugs from the dresser.

Laura paused in the doorway, her eyes briefly meeting Louise's. Then she shrugged, before turning to follow Becky upstairs. Louise stared after her, only half hearing as Ken continued teasing James. She sensed that any reconciliation with Ken's elder daughter was further away than ever.

Getting up early had never been a problem for James, not even when he'd had a paper round and football training to fit in each morning before school. He liked being awake while the rest of the family was sleeping. The house was quiet and still, and he could work on his music. It was almost daylight now, the blackbirds in the pear tree outside his window were whistling and calling.

James closed his composition notebook and switched off the bedside lamp, stretching out on his back, his arms folded behind his head. To his surprise, he had realised he missed playing football. Although the season was over, the team still had to train and practise. It was that commitment he was relieved not to have. He didn't regret being dropped from the team.

Except that his father would be disappointed when he found out. James stared at the ceiling and sighed. He'd been putting off telling Dad. Waiting for the right moment, he told himself. But the right moment just never seemed to happen.

James listened as the grandfather clock at the foot of the stairs chimed the quarter hour. It was too early to get up yet. He didn't need to be at the Green Dairy for another hour yet. Deliveries were later on Sundays. It was thanks to Charlotte that James had got the job helping one of the regular milkmen on his round.

Charlotte's brother, Simon, had given the job up to go back-packing in Algeria, and Charlotte had put a word in with her father. Mr Green's family had owned the dairy for generations.

James hadn't received his first wage packet yet, but he already knew exactly how he would spend it! It would be nice to be able to take Charlotte out occasionally. Not that they were going steady, as Dad called it, but they were good friends and James like her a lot.

Then there were books he wanted, and

new music … things he would never ask Dad for money to buy. Yes, having some money of his own would be great. Especially if his exam grades were good enough and he did get into music college.

James swung his legs off the bed and got up. There was no point in planning, or even thinking, that far ahead, he told himself as he had a shower. He had to get through his A-Levels first. And despite having written to Manchester almost two weeks ago, he still hadn't received a reply from the Royal Northern College of Music.

James sprinted noiselessly downstairs, jumping over the three that creaked and towelling his wet hair as he went. At the bottom, he caught sight of his reflection in the tall wall mirror – and grimaced. Dabbing the trickle of blood on his smooth cheek with the towel, he realised it had been a mistake to shave. It wasn't as though there'd been much in the way of bristle, but he'd managed to nick himself anyhow. Now he'd have to stand up in front of Charlotte, and the entire church congregation, and play a violin solo with little bits of tissue paper stuck to his face!

James hurried into the kitchen and tossed the towel into the wash basket. Laura must already be out walking Smokey, because his lead was gone from the hook on the back of the door. Of course, she'd have an early start today, too. It was her week for doing the church flowers. And after church, she'd be going into work for a few hours to help with the traditional Lancashire lunch that Monk's Inn served on Sundays.

James poured a glass of orange juice and cut two uneven slices of bread for toast. It still seemed odd to come down in the mornings and not see Laura moving quietly about the kitchen, the table set for breakfast and the lunch-boxes packed and ready. He buttered his toast, spreading it thickly with home-made gooseberry jam. Louise wasn't accustomed to early rising. She'd admitted that her notion of breakfast was strong black coffee and a quick flip through the Hong Kong newspapers.

James smiled, recalling the chaos of those first few days. The whole family would get in each other's way, scurrying round the kitchen at the last minute. Anything that could get burned or spilled invariably did! But Louise never got rattled. Somehow everything got done in the end.

And it all seemed to be working out, because mornings were pretty calm and organised now.

James made himself another piece of toast. He'd noticed that Laura had been keeping very much in the background lately. Cheerfully helping, but careful not to get in the way. But what was she really feeling? James couldn't even guess.

They'd always been so close, yet his sister hadn't said a word. James finished his juice and put on his jacket. He and Laura just didn't talk to each other the way they used to. They used to discuss everything together when Dad was away at sea. More and more, he found himself wondering if Laura was as cheerful and settled as she appeared.

After church, Becky was eager to show her father the foals in McCobb's meadow.

Ken turned to Louise. 'Coming with us, love? McCobb's is only about half a mile from David's market garden. We can pop over and say hello. I'm sure he'll be pleased to give you a guided tour. David's not the sort of man to boast, but he's done wonders with the place. Not just the land, the mill, too. It'd been derelict since the Thirties.'

'Perhaps another day,' Louise replied, thinking it would be nice for Ken and Becky to have a few hours alone together. 'I want to get everything ready for this afternoon.'

'We're not expecting royalty!' Ken protested with a laugh. 'Just the family for Sunday tea. Mind you, if Alex Fairbrass is coming...' he glanced wryly at James as he joined them. 'Maybe you should give the silver an extra polish! Alex thinks he is royalty, isn't that right, Jimmy?'

'Don't mind what Dad said,' James commented as he and Louise strolled home from the village after church. 'Uncle Alex is all right. He and Dad just seem to rub each other up the wrong way, that's all. They never actually quarrel, they just sort of ... of...'

'Annoy one another?' Louise suggested amiably.

James laughed, and nodded. 'It's Auntie Helen I feel sorry for. She's the one who usually has to smooth things over.'

'Helen is your mum's younger sister, isn't she? I'm looking forward to meeting her,' Louise remarked, as she pushed open Spryglass's weathered gate. 'And your cousins.'

'Well, Diane'll be here,' James answered, unlocking the front door and standing aside for Louise to go in. 'Even though they've moved away, she still goes to my school, and she told me she'd definitely be coming this afternoon. But I wouldn't count on Ashley. He has an important job at Liverpool Museum – and he's a consultant with an auction house in Chester. Ash is away most weekends viewing furniture and paintings and so on.' He paused, waiting.

Louise had stopped at the kitchen door. 'I know it's family tradition to have Sunday tea here in the kitchen,' she commented. 'But since this is the first dry and sunny day we've had all week, how do you feel about eating outdoors?'

'Eeee, this is the life!' Dan Jessup sighed contentedly. The family had just enjoyed a delicious tea in Spryglass's sea-facing, sun-filled garden. 'And thank you for my present,' he went on, nonchalantly adjusting the stylish tie Ken and Louise had brought from Hong Kong. 'I'll wear this when I collect my pension and impress the postmistress. She's one of my girlfriends, y'know.'

'She won't be able to resist you in that tie, Dan!' Ken grinned, glancing up to where Alex was sitting between Nancy and Laura on the shady porch.

'Hope that Chinese paperweight was all right for you, Alex. I couldn't get a wee one!' He turned to Louise to explain. 'Alex has a factory on the old Dock Road, where the overhead railway used to be – Gulliver's Toys. So how is the water-pistol business then, Alex?'

'Hard. Like earning a living from any other kind of business,' his brother-in-law returned shortly. 'You'll find life ashore a great deal tougher than sailing all over the place without a care–'

'Oh, don't let's talk shop!' Helen interrupted mildly, giving Louise an apologetic look. 'It's so nice, the whole family being together for once. I'm only sorry Ashley couldn't be here, too. He's in St Anne's viewing a collection of military medals an old gentleman wants to sell.' There was pride in her voice.

James heard a poorly smothered giggle, and Diane flopped down beside him on the grass. He'd been sitting in the shade of the apple tree, preoccupied with budgeting the proceeds of his milk round.

'Ash is in St Anne's all right,' she whispered slyly. 'What Mum and Dad don't know, is that he's taken Cindy Sharples with him! I listened in on the extension when he was phoning her to make the arrangements!'

'You would.' James sounded disinterested, scribbling some figures into the back of his notebook.

Diane frowned at him, disappointed that her news had met with so little response. 'Have you heard from the music college yet?' she asked after a minute. 'About getting an audition?' She now had James' full attention.

'Why not just shout my private business to the whole village!'

'Oh, sorry. I didn't realise it was a big secret!' She pulled a contrite face.

'It's not a secret, it's just private!' James said firmly. 'And you shouldn't have been eavesdropping when Charlotte and I were discussing it!' He got up, shoved his hands into the pockets of his jeans and wandered down the garden and out of the gate on to the shore. The tide was ebbing, quiet and smooth with barely a ripple.

James narrowed his eyes against the almost harsh brightness of the sun. Grandad was right about this fine weather only being a respite. The sky above the Welsh hills was ominously dark, a sure warning of more storms to come.

The torrential rain, driven by a gale-force wind, had finally ceased shortly before dawn. By breakfast time, only a dry north-westerly still gusted around Spryglass, tearing the remaining blossom from the trees.

Laura was relieved that her father and Louise hadn't had to cancel their planned shopping trip to Southport.

Louise needed warmer, more serviceable clothing. Although the two women were not the same size, Laura had loaned her a mackintosh, just in case of another downpour.

Clearing the breakfast dishes, Laura planned her day. She wasn't due at Monk's Inn until noon, so, once James and Becky got off to school, she'd have the whole morning – and the house – to herself. There'd been no chance to do any proper baking since Louise arrived. But now she had the time, why not make a treat for tea?

The sound of her father's annoyed voice sent her hurrying into the dining-room. She knew at once what the cross words were about. James was standing dejectedly, schoolbag over his shoulder, his attempts at explanations falling on to deaf ears.

'You had a responsibility to your coach, to your team-mates, Jimmy!' Ken declared, his eyes drilling into the boy. 'You've let them down! And why did I have to ask you Jimmy? Why didn't you tell me?'

'I was going to tell you–' James insisted wretchedly.

'When? Next week? Next month?' Ken's voice was sarcastic. 'You have to work to get anywhere in this life. You can't afford to lose chances by being too lazy to–'

'It wasn't like that, Dad!' Laura interrupted, unable to hold her tongue any longer. 'James did try to keep up with the practices, but he's had so much studying–'

'This is between Jimmy and me,' Ken cut in shortly. 'Let your brother speak for himself.'

'What good will that do?' James blurted, his face taut and white, as he glared across at his father. 'You never listen to me. Never! You don't hear anyone but yourself!' He turned on his heel and strode from the room.

Ken immediately began to follow. 'Jimmy! Don't you–'

Louise laid a restraining hand on his arm. 'Why not leave him be for now?' she suggested quietly. 'James and Becky have to go to school soon, and we're on our way out. Wouldn't it be better to talk this evening?'

Ken took a deep breath, his face grim. But he nodded, exhaling in exasperation. 'Yes, that makes sense. I'll just say cheerio to Becky. Then we'll get off for our train...'

When the front door closed behind Ken and Louise, Laura went to look for James. He was standing forlornly in the garden.

'Away you go to school, now.' Laura gave him an encouraging push as Becky came running towards them. 'And let me get on with my baking!'

Working alone in the quiet kitchen, Laura's thoughts strayed again and again to David. She hadn't seen him for ages. She'd been furious with him when they'd argued, believing he was not only wrong, but unfair, too. Now it didn't seem to matter who was to blame for the row. All she wanted was to see him again, be with him.

Laura suddenly made up her mind to swallow her pride and apologise. Now she waited with growing impatience for the baking to be finished, so she could be on her way to Riverside Mill.

A Crushing Blow

Drifts of wind-blown sand, broken branches, and other debris from the previous night's storm lay strewn across the lane. Laura had to dismount and walk her bicycle, manoeuvring between puddles and ruts of thick mud. As the mill's distinctive, crooked chimney came into sight she stopped, stunned by the devastation.

The last time she'd been here, neat fields had been green with growing vegetables. Now sheets of floodwater extended from hedgerow to hedgerow. The murky surface was occasionally broken by the straggling tips of plants and seedlings floated forlornly, swept from their boxes. The cold-frames were smashed, their contents crushed and broken. The greenhouses were a tangled mass of broken glass and splintered timbers.

Laura's horrified eyes at last caught a glimpse of David, emerging round the side of the mill. There was a coiled rope slung over his shoulder and his face was lined with exhaustion. The relief that he was safe almost overwhelmed her.

'David!' Laura ran to him.

David caught her in his arms, holding her

tight, his face buried in her hair. 'It's all over,' he mumbled huskily. 'Finished. There's no way I can–'

'Don't even *think* that!' Laura replied fiercely, holding his face in both her hands. 'The mill can be saved. We'll do it together!'

David stared at her silently, the moments ticking past. 'That's impossible,' he said tightly, a note of anger edging into his voice. 'Don't you realise...?' Taking her wrists in his hands, he slowly moved Laura away from him, so they were standing apart. 'It's too late. We can't get married now! Just take a look round!' David's eyes were full of despair.

But Laura couldn't tear her gaze from his face. He was despondent. Broken. His hopes and dreams, all he'd planned and worked so long and hard for, suddenly in ruins. Her every feeling, every thought was for him. Nothing else mattered. Not the devastation around her. Not the embarrassment of having asked David to marry her. Or the humiliation of his blunt refusal.

David was usually so strong and decisive and, yes, vital was the word. Brimming with plans and ideas, and with such a passion for life and for his work. As soon as she'd met him, Laura had felt drawn to this proud, fiercely independent man, whose smile could make her feel so special.

Now David stood before her, every ounce

of energy and spirit knocked out of him. He was unshaven, his clothes soaked, his dark eyes underlined by even darker shadows. Had he been working the whole night? Battling alone against the howling wind and cold, blinding rain in a vain, hopeless fight to save what was already beyond saving?

Not long ago, Laura had depended on David completely. Now he was defeated and vulnerable. Now he needed her. She took a tentative step towards him, her fear of rebuff overwhelmed by her desire to comfort. Almost shyly, she slipped her arms about his waist and hugged him.

This time, David did not push her away. Laura felt some of the tension ebbing from his body, and moved closer against him, resting her cheek against his shoulder.

'I love you, David,' she murmured.

David's breath caught in his throat, and she raised her face to look at him.

'That's the first time you've ever said that.' He exhaled slowly. To have heard Laura say those words, even twenty-four hours ago, would have meant everything to him. Now it was too late. Just as her finally deciding to marry him had come too late.

Suddenly David was filled with bitterness. He drew away from her, staring out across the flooded fields. He'd lost everything. There'd be debts he couldn't pay. Orders that couldn't be filled. And what of the mortgage on the mill? Suppose it was re-possessed?

Now he was angry. He'd worked hard, done his best. All for nothing. In less than an hour, the storm had wiped out years of effort, and left him with nothing! No liveli-hood, no future. Not even a home to offer Laura.

'I'd better get back to work,' he said tersely, stooping to retrieve the rope he'd dropped. 'I have to get a tarpaulin on the roof before the rain starts again.'

Pushing her wind-blown hair from her eyes, Laura followed him round the corner – then stopped in dismay. There must be hundreds, perhaps thousands of pounds' worth of damage to the roof and upper-storey wall above the mill-wheel. The round window with its thick, almost green, glass was gone completely.

'It was the window coming in that woke me last night,' David commented. 'My guitar was underneath a heap of rubble. When I dug it out there wasn't so much as a broken string,' he concluded with grim humour. 'How's that for irony?'

Laura could scarcely speak. 'David – you look terrible,' she murmured after a minute. 'You're so exhausted you can hardly stand. And I don't suppose you've eaten anything either. You must take a break!'

'I can't!' he answered sharply. 'Maybe it's

71

hopeless, but I have to keep trying. I can't just do nothing!'

'Don't you think I understand that?' Laura returned gently. 'But when you're rested and thinking straight, things might not look quite so bad. Please come inside. I'll make you something to eat–'

'There's no need for that, Laura,' he said flatly. 'Shouldn't you be at work?'

'Not for a while yet,' she replied, checking her watch.

'Besides,' David was saying, glancing at the darkening sky. 'I have to get that tarpaulin battened on.'

'All right. You do that, while I get a meal started.' Laura smiled encouragingly. 'When you're finished, come in and we'll talk while I cook. We'll sort things out – you'll see!'

Despite Laura's unshakable optimism, as David worked on the roof, he could find no answers to his problem. The same questions had been going round and round in his head all night. His mind was weary trying to make some sense of it all.

He'd walked out of his father's house eight years ago, with little more than the clothes he stood up in, a few books that had belonged to his mother, and his precious guitar. He'd only left school a few months before and hadn't a clue what he wanted to do with his life.

What he didn't want was to become the kind of man his father was. Not for him a life of betrayal and deception! He'd left what remained of his family, his friends and Polkerris. And never gone back. He'd picked fruit and hops, laboured in the fields, even worked in a foundry to pay for his horticultural training. What little free time he had was spent hiking the length and breadth of the country looking for a place where he could belong.

A few years later, when he was working for a large-scale co-operative of organic cereal growers, David came upon Riverside Mill. It had stood empty since the Thirties – and even then it must have been an austere, cheerless place to live. No electricity. No gas. No plumbing. Only cold water from a single tap. But David knew that some day it would make a proper home...

And the land! At first, he couldn't believe his luck! Uncultivated for over fifty years, the rich, dark earth was packed with vital nutrients and mineral salts. With growing excitement, he did countless soil tests – it was perfect for a market garden producing organic fruit and vegetables!

He'd scraped together the money to acquire the mill. Then for more than a year David slept in a sleeping-bag on the floor beside the great millstones. Rarely setting foot beyond the mill, he'd worked sixteen-hour days.

By the end of summer, and starting to see some profits, David finally turned his attentions to the mill-house itself. Made it sound and weatherproof. Swept the chimneys and rebuilt the stone fireplaces. Got connected to all the modern amenities. And scoured auction sales for furniture.

He'd been rather self-consciously buying cushions at the Sandford Christmas Fayre the day he'd met Laura. Walking home across the snow-covered village green, he'd met the first woman he'd ever wanted to share his life with. She was playing in the snow with a little girl.

But Laura wasn't free. Oh, she wasn't married or engaged; she didn't even have a boyfriend. She was just devoted to her family. Caring for James and Becky and Spryglass always came first. David admired her for it, loved her for it ... but sometimes he couldn't help resenting it, too.

He'd never tried to hide his feelings for Laura, yet she'd always kept him at arm's length. There always seemed to be a good reason for their not being together. For not making plans to marry. Then, when her father remarried and came ashore, Laura turned down his proposal in no uncertain terms... He was beginning to wonder if she loved him at all.

The house felt cold and damp when Laura

74

entered. The first thing she did was make a fire in the long living-room. As soon as it began to crackle, the mill seemed brighter and cheerier. Laura slipped off her coat, and hesitated by the phone. It was getting late, but she couldn't just walk out and leave David. Quickly she phoned Monk's Inn and explained to Mrs Lancaster what had happened. Could she come in later?

'I'll make up the lost time, of course,' she concluded.

'Don't be silly. Frank and I wouldn't hear of it,' Beattie Lancaster replied kindly. She and her husband had been Riverside's first customers, placing a large, regular order for fruit and vegetables. The elderly couple had come to know David well, and liked him. 'It's not as though we're rushed off our feet here,' she went on. 'It sounds as if you're needed more where you are. This must be a terrible blow for David.'

Despite Mrs Lancaster suggesting she take the whole afternoon off, Laura promised she'd be in later.

As she hung up, she was reflecting that Monk's Inn was awfully quiet these days. Nothing like it usually was at this time of year.

In the kitchen, the range David had never been able to replace had gone out and was stone cold. Laura quickly cleaned and lit it, but nothing could be cooked until it heated up. Waiting, she saw the open books and invoices spread out over the let-down lid of the bureau. David had obviously spent the previous evening tackling Riverside's accounts. She felt a pang of remorse. Until their recent quarrel, she'd done all the paperwork.

Sifting through the papers, Laura saw that everything was up to date. She did some calculations. David should be able to tick over until at least the middle of next month. By then, he should have received the money from his insurance claim. She began to leaf through the pigeon-holes for the relevant documents.

It was raining heavily again when David came in. When he saw the warmly welcoming kitchen, with its glowing range and hearty breakfast waiting to be served, his face lit up.

'I really didn't want you to do this, Laura,' he said quietly, then added with a rueful smile, 'but I'm grateful – thanks.'

'It's only breakfast!' She returned his smile. 'Not a banquet!'

'Well, it looks good to me.' He ran a grimy hand through his wet, tangled hair. 'Have I time for a wash and shave?'

When he came back downstairs, clean and dry, Laura set the plates on the kitchen table. 'I've looked over the paperwork, David,' she said gently. 'You're dreadfully under-insured.'

'Couldn't afford the premiums,' he answered simply, taking a sip of coffee from the big, earthenware mug. 'I know I'm in trouble.'

'Ye-es,' Laura admitted slowly. She'd been racking her brains for a way to help Riverside survive. If she was in trouble, she'd turn to her family. But David ... she knew so little about his past. Hadn't he mentioned his father was a Cornish fisherman? And something about two sisters older than him? She suspected that, no matter how desperate his situation became, David would never ask for their help.

'What you need–' she went on thoughtfully '–is a quick crop. Something that ... that...'

'Grows fast, preferably underwater,' he supplied with a faint smile. 'And makes lots of money very, very quickly?'

Laura shrugged apologetically.

'No, you're absolutely right. That's exactly what I need.' David took more hot toast and buttered it. 'I don't have many ideas at the moment. All I know is that Riverside is mine. I'll do everything in my power to save it!'

Laura was glad to see David more like his usual confident self.

'You're sure I can't drive you into the village? David asked, when Laura was ready to leave. She shook her head, glancing out to the bright sky. 'There's no need – the rain's gone off.'

'Mmm, I must call in at Monk's Inn myself,' David commented soberly. 'Tell the Lancasters I shan't be able to supply the hotel's order.'

'They'll realise that,' Laura told him. 'But I can pass on a message, if you like?'

'No, Beattie and Frank stuck by me through all the teething troubles when Riverside first opened. I want to have a word with them personally. I need to go over to McCobb's and see Lyndsey, too,' he added as an afterthought. 'She's just put in a big order for the barn dance supper.'

Lyndsey McCobb's annual barn dance in aid of the local animal shelter had become a popular event in Sandford. People of all ages went and enjoyed themselves.

'Auntie Helen is organizing the barbecue. And Gran and I'll be doing some baking!' Laura smiled. 'And this year, Becky is going to cook up a tray of her fudge whirls!'

'I'd buy a ticket just to get my share of those!' David grinned as he walked Laura to the gate. 'Is Louise helping, too?'

'I've no idea,' she answered stiffly, her face set. 'I shouldn't think a country barn dance and supper would interest her much.'

David glanced at her and the vague doubts that had been nagging at the back of his mind came into focus. Would Laura have come back to him – wanted to marry him – if life with Louise hadn't been so difficult?

At the gate, Laura half turned. David was studying her with a brooding expression in his dark eyes that she'd never seen before.

It stayed with her all afternoon as she checked the freshly-laundered linen in her cubby-hole of an office at Monk's Inn. David hadn't kissed her goodbye. Usually he was eager to be with her, reluctant to let her leave. Yet today, they'd parted without even a caress. Without David saying when he would see her again.

Laura methodically ticked off the items of linen on her list one by one. Then she folded it neatly into the basket, trying to ignore how cold her hands were, and how they were trembling. She'd felt so sure of David. Certain he loved and wanted her. It had never occurred to her that he'd be the one to end it.

The jaunty ringing of the brass bell on the reception desk jarred Laura from the unhappiness of her thoughts. Hurrying out into the lobby, she found a fair-haired young man wandering about looking at the watercolours on the walls. He was wearing a loose-fitting summer shirt and jeans, and a motorcycle helmet dangled from one hand.

'May I help you?'

He turned and smiled at her, sauntering across to the desk.

'Evening! You've got a room for me, I believe? I'm not certain exactly how long I'll be staying.' He watched Laura reach for a registration card. 'Best book me in for a week to begin with. My name's Shaun Pembridge.'

A few days later, James was waiting outside the village shop for Becky. Absently he gazed at the window display of chocolates and sweets. Later that evening, he was taking Charlotte into Liverpool to see 'Hamlet' at the Playhouse. It was part of their school syllabus, but this evening wouldn't be like their usual trips to the library. For a start they were having a meal in the theatre restaurant first. More like a date. A proper date. Their first...

'Becky, if you were a girl–' James began vaguely when his sister came out of the sweetie shop. 'Would you like chocolates?'

'I am a girl, and I do like chocolates!' Becky retorted indignantly. 'I bet Charlotte does, too!' she added impishly.

James looked at the prices in dismay. He'd needed to save hard just to afford the tickets and dinner. 'As for the bow ... can I borrow one of your hair ribbons?'

'Hurry up!' Becky urged. 'I want to show Laura my necklace.'

Becky's class had spent the afternoon cutting up egg boxes and turning them into flowers. Becky had strung her vividly-painted flowers into a long necklace. As she rushed ahead of James into Monk's Inn, Laura was in the lobby pinning up a notice about McCobb's barn dance.

'Laura – look!' Becky cried excitedly, holding out the necklace. 'Look what I made!'

'It's lovely!' Laura dropped to her knees so her face was near Becky's. 'It's the nicest necklace I've ever–'

'Becky made it for Louise!' James cut in hastily, his eyes meeting Laura's. 'She wanted to ask you if Louise will like it. I'm sure she will – aren't you?'

'Oh – yes. Of course, she will!' Laura reassured, grateful James had interrupted when he did. Becky had always given her the things she made at school... With a tinge of sadness she realised that another of the old ties had been broken.

'Louise will love it.' Laura walked out into the hot sunshine with James and Becky. 'You just wait and–'

'There's David!' Becky shouted suddenly, breaking away and running towards the churchyard.

David had been earning extra money jobbing for the church-warden.

'Watch the road, Becky!' James called, returning David's wave of greeting.

'Laura – hang on!' James halted her as she turned to go back inside Monk's Inn. 'Last

81

night I heard Dad asking when you and David planned to get married.'

'I've already explained that, with the trouble at Riverside, we'd postponed making plans,' Laura responded warily. 'It's only sensible.'

'True – and Dad accepted it,' James went on carefully. 'But he doesn't know how things used to be between you. David was like one of the family. At Spryglass every morning for breakfast, and most evenings for tea. Now he hardly ever comes to the house, and when he does, it's when he's fairly certain you won't be there. I've watched you with him at Riverside. Oh, you worked hard to help him clear up, but you scarcely spoke to each other. And, just now, you didn't even wave to him!' James looked at his sister with concern. 'What's wrong, Laura?'

'I don't want to talk about it,' she said miserably. 'I can't.'

James touched her arm sympathetically. 'I'm really sorry,' he murmured, frowning as he searched for the right words. 'Laura ... when Dad and I were helping rebuild the glasshouses, he insisted David come round for tea tonight. I could see he didn't want to, but you know what Dad's like. He just wouldn't take no for an answer. David couldn't refuse without being rude.' He hesitated uneasily. 'I thought you should know…'

'I'll pop in to Gran's after work,' Laura

commented after a minute. 'I won't be home for tea.'

'Since you're eating out, it's just David, Becky and me for tea then,' Louise commented later to James, taking a huge jug of freshly-squeezed orange juice and adding ice cubes.

They were in the cool kitchen and she was wearing the flower necklace Becky had given her.

She'd accepted it with such pleasure that James had watched his little sister lose some of her shyness.

'Have you time for some of this?' Louise gestured with the jug.

'Yes. I don't have to get changed for ages yet. Where's Dad?'

'Out with your grandfather. Nancy's standing in for one of the other hospital visitors and Dan didn't want to spend such a gorgeous evening alone in the flat. He said he was off to collect coal – from the beach.' Louise shrugged, perplexed. 'Perhaps I misunderstood?'

'No, that'd be right,' James said, taking the day's post from the dresser. 'Grandad reckons there's a coal seam under the river. After certain tides, a lot of coal gets washed up. I'm glad Dad's gone with him. Grandad really shouldn't be...' His voice tailed off as he came to a long, slim envelope.

It was postmarked Manchester. From the Royal Northern College of Music. He stared at it. He'd nearly given up hope of getting a reply.

Louise glanced at him. 'What's wrong?'

James didn't answer at first. He slit open the envelope, withdrawing a single sheet of paper and scanning the few typewritten lines. He hadn't told anyone – not even Laura – that he'd applied for an audition. Wordlessly, he passed the letter to Louise.

'Oh, James!' Congratulations!' she exclaimed, giving him a hug.

'It's only an audition.' He grinned. 'I may not be good enough to get a place.'

'You will,' she returned confidently. 'You have talent – it must be developed.'

'I wish Dad thought so.' James' face was solemn. 'He has all these plans for me! Getting back into the football team. Going to university. Having a career in professional sport... He'll hit the roof!'

'Choose your moment. Then talk to him quietly,' Louise suggested. 'Since you've been working together at Riverside he's realised you're no longer a child. A young man is expected to have ideas of his own. You may be surprised at his reaction.'

James was unconvinced. His father wasn't given to changing his mind.

'I'll carry that,' he offered, folding the letter into his shirt pocket and taking the heavy tray from Louise's hands. 'You won't say anything, will you?'

'Of course not. It's your news.' She smiled at him over her shoulder as he followed her out into the garden. 'Thank you for sharing it with me.'

James was too preoccupied to join in the light-hearted conversation in Spryglass's sunny back garden. Presently, he went up to change for his date with Charlotte.

From the landing window, he spotted Laura coming towards the front gate. She was earlier than he'd expected but, of course, she wouldn't have got any answer at Gran's flat. Checking that he had both wallet and theatre tickets, James went downstairs, and into the kitchen.

'Laura?'

She was standing absolutely still, just inside the open back door, looking out to the garden. James could see past her to where Louise was sitting on the lawn, laughing and chatting with Becky and David.

Slowly, Laura turned around. James was shocked to see that her cheeks were wet with tears. He'd hardly ever seen Laura cry before.

'I've lost him, Jamie,' she murmured brokenly. 'And I want him back – so much!'

James didn't know what to do or say.

How could he comfort her?

Finally, he just drew his sister away into

the privacy of the living-room. Then, putting his arms around her, he patted her shoulder, exactly as he would Becky.

Shaun Pembridge

The clock in the village church was striking one, and the moon was washing Spryglass's garden with silvery light when James silently let himself into the house.

'And what time do you call this to come sneaking in?' Ken demanded, his voice uncharacteristically harsh. 'Where have you been until now, my lad?'

James tensed. In the shadows of the unlit kitchen, he hadn't noticed his father sitting at the table.

'I walked Charlotte home,' he answered evenly. He hadn't done anything wrong, and resented being made to feel as though he had. 'I did say I'd be back late, Dad.'

'Ah, I'm only having you on, Jimmy!' Ken grinned, raising a conciliatory hand. 'I don't remember much about being seventeen – but I do remember how a ten-minute walk can take three hours! And I wasn't waiting for you,' he continued, getting up to refill his cup. 'I couldn't sleep and didn't want to disturb Louise by tossing and turning. Want one?' He held up the teapot.

'No, thanks–' James hesitated. Amazingly, he'd almost forgotten about having to tell his father of the music college audition. 'Er – yes – OK then.' He pulled back a chair and sat down.

'I want to talk to you, Dad.'

'Fire away,' Ken returned genially, setting down the mugs. 'I'm in the mood for listening.'

James met his father's gaze levelly. 'Dad – after my 'A'-levels are over, I'm finished with school. I'm not going on to Liverpool University like you want.' James took a deep breath. 'I want to have a career in music, Dad. Become a professional musician.'

'A man has to make his way in the real world, Jimmy,' Ken told him practically. 'It's a hard place if you've no skills and no qualifications.'

'I would have qualifications, Dad,' James replied, with no trace of the silent, immature sullenness this kind of conversation had previously provoked. 'After three years, I'd get my degree – Graduate of the Royal Schools of Music.'

Ken was watching his son from across the table. James' face looked very young and earnest in the moonlight. Suddenly, Ken recalled something of what it was like to be seventeen, filled with enthusiasm and impossible dreams...

Would it do any real harm to let Jimmy attend this audition? It might even do a bit of good – help get this musical nonsense out of his system.

'All right, Jimmy. I'll tell you what we'll do,' he said evenly. 'I'll let you go to the audition – on one condition. If you fail, that's it. Finished. The end of any talk of you being a musician.'

'All right.' James shrugged in a burst of bravado. 'You have my promise. But I won't need to keep it. Because I'm going to pass that audition, Dad!'

Ken was so dumbfounded by James' confidence that he didn't say another word as his son left the kitchen. He got up and took the mugs to the sink, admitting a grudging new respect.

'So here you are!'

Ken glanced around as Louise padded, barefoot, into the kitchen.

'I woke up and you weren't there!' She put her arms about his waist, resting her head sleepily against his shoulder blades. 'It's almost two o'clock. What are you going, darling?'

'You won't believe it.' He turned around, wrapping his arms about her. 'Jimmy's just told me he's–' Ken paused, watching her. 'You know already, don't you?'

She nodded. 'I was here when he opened the letter.'

'And you said nothing? Didn't you think I had a right to know?'

'James wanted to speak to you himself,'

she replied calmly. 'I felt obliged to respect his wishes.'

In the slivery light, Louise's face was as young and earnest as Jimmy's had been. And, with a jolt of realization, Ken suddenly knew why she and his son got on so well together. Instinctively, he tightened his arms about her. The difference in their ages had never mattered before – he hardly ever thought about it. But suddenly Ken was conscious of every single one of the years that separated him from his wife.

'Since I left Hong Kong, I've really missed my exercise class,' Louise commented, changing the subject tactfully, slipping her arm through his. 'When James took me to enroll in the library, I saw a notice about fitness classes starting next month in the village hall,' she went on. 'Helen and I are going to go.'

'Helen?' Ken asked in surprise. 'Well, if that's what you want... I'm pleased you're friendly. She's a fine woman.' Ken had long held a deep affection for his mild-natured sister-in-law. 'For all she and Alex are well off, I don't think she's too happy just now.'

'She hasn't confided in me,' Louise remarked quietly. 'But I think she and Alex are maybe having problems.'

'Yes – and Alex is the main one!' Ken returned scathingly. 'How did you talk Helen into this keep-fit scene? She's such a sensible, down-to-earth sort – it's not her cup of tea at all!'

'Helen's extremely keen.' Louise laughed. 'We're both looking forward to the classes very much! To begin with, we're taking yoga and dance.'

'I suppose I should come too.' Ken ruefully patted his middle. 'I've put on weight since I came ashore. If I get any fatter, I'll need new jeans!'

'You'll need a few more clothes before you start your job. We can go shopping together.' Louise smiled, putting her arms around Ken's waist and giving him a hug. 'And you're not fat, darling. You're just cuddly!'

Laura nipped the faded flowers from the trailing fuchsia and, carrying the heavy basket carefully, headed for the front door of Monk's Inn. But she quickly drew back into the shadow of the porch as David Hale's van rumbled by. She watched from the side window as he parked farther along the street. He carried several boxes of salad produce into the greengrocer's, before continuing through the village and away towards Riverside Mill. It seemed strange that he no longer stopped for a chat...

Laura hung the flower basket on the cast-iron bracket outside the front door. In the early-morning sun, the flaking plaster of the inn's walls and the faded paintwork were more noticeable than ever.

It was such a shame – and not Beattie and Frank Lancaster's fault – that Monk's Inn was becoming run-down and dilapidated. The elderly couple worked as hard as ever, but the hotel just wasn't doing so well any more. Even now, in mid-summer, Mr Pembridge and the elderly Misses Forwood were the only guests.

Laura returned indoors. It distressed her to see Monk's Inn looking so shabby. The old coaching inn was so much a part of the village – and of her childhood memories.

The Lancasters had been kind to her. They'd taken her on when she was barely sixteen, patiently teaching her about catering and running a busy little hotel. Beattie and Frank had never changed – Monk's Inn certainly had!

Laura was back in her office when Beattie Lancaster looked in.

'Frank and I'll be off shortly. Mrs Middleton is seeing us at nine sharp.' Beattie fiddled with the white collar of her neat navy two-piece. 'Thanks for looking after things while we're in Liverpool. It's good of you to give up your day off.'

'I'm glad to help,' Laura replied quietly. She was fond of the Lancasters, and had willingly agreed to help when the couple's accountant had asked them for a meeting. Beattie looked so agitated, Laura felt she had to say something else. 'I – I'm sure everything will be all right, Mrs Lancaster.'

When the Lancasters got back, they went straight to their private sitting-room. Both looked solemn, and Beattie was watery-eyed.

Laura waited ten minutes, then prepared a tray of tea and took it to them.

The inn's books were spread out across the table in front of them. Beattie hastily pushed a damp handkerchief into her sleeve as Laura entered the cluttered, old-fashioned room.

'Sit down, dear.' She sniffed, exchanging a glance with Frank. 'You've been with us a long while. It's only fair you know what's happening.'

'Our meeting with Mrs Middleton was pretty grim,' Frank Lancaster began in his forthright fashion. 'We must make even more economies! We might even have to let some of the staff go.'

Laura stared in consternation. She'd realised things were bad, but–

'Your job's safe!' Beattie put in hastily. 'You're practically family. As long as Frank and I are at Monk's Inn, there'll be a job for you.'

Despite the Lancasters' reassurances, Laura was shaken when she left the sitting-room. She hurried into the lobby.

'Sorry!' Shaun Pembridge almost cannoned into her as she turned the corner. 'My fault! I wasn't looking where I was going!'

'Neither was I,' Laura conceded with a polite smile.

'Actually, I'd like a word–' Shaun broke off, bending slightly to look at her face. 'Are you all right? You look a bit upset.'

'It's nothing, really.' She forced another smile. 'How may I help you?'

'What? Oh, yes… I've got a bit of a problem.' Shaun set the gaily gift-wrapped box he was carrying down on to the lobby desk. 'My elder sister lives up at Hesketh Bank. It's her daughter's birthday, and as a treat, I usually take Pippa out. I've missed her last two birthdays because I was working in Saudi, so I wanted this outing to be really good. She's mad on tennis right now. Wants to go to the ladies singles Final at the Wirral Tournament. She's even invited three of her pals along!'

'So you want me to get tickets?'

'Tickets are the least of my worries! It's the girls! One excitable nine-year-old is bad enough. But four! And Pippa's pal, Donna, apparently gets car sick… I do realise I've an awful nerve asking,' he gazed at Laura hopefully, 'but would you come with us? Please?' he finished a shade desperately.

'It is my day off…' Laura looked straight back at him, not sure what to do.

Shaun Pembridge was in his twenties. He

seemed nice enough, always bright and breezy, with a smile for everyone. During the time he'd been staying at Monk's Inn, Laura had found him polite and likeable ... but that was no measure of his ability to cope with four children!

Laura made up her mind all at once. 'Yes, I'll come. Thank you.'

'Thank you!' He heaved a great sigh of gratitude. 'You've saved my life! I haven't brought my car up from Staffordshire yet. I've been doing all my sightseeing by motor-bike. So can you arrange for me to hire one?'

'No problem.' Laura was already leafing through the index of telephone numbers. 'I'll get on to it right away.'

'Super! And thanks again.' Shaun picked up his package and started for the stairs. 'Oh, is twelve-thirty all right for you?'

Laura nodded. 'Twelve-thirty will be fine.'

'Well, that went well!' Shaun declared that evening, when the last of the little girls had been safely delivered home. He and Laura were just beginning the drive back to Sandford. 'What a day, eh?'

'We had a lovely time!' Laura protested mildly, smiling. 'The tennis was exciting – and so was the strawberry and champagne tea!'

Shaun glanced sidelong at her. 'You're really good with kids,' he commented. 'I'm surprised you don't work with them. Teacher, nanny – something like that.'

'Actually, I would've liked to teach,' Laura confessed. 'Little ones, you know.'

'So why didn't you?'

'Oh, I wanted to stay at home.' She smiled. 'Be close to my family.'

'Ah, yes,' Shaun murmured. 'Mrs Lancaster mentioned you'd lost your mother when you were still very young.'

For a while, Laura had almost forgotten about the problems at Monk's Inn. Now they came flooding back. Her face shadowed.

'Can't you tell me what's upsetting you, Laura?' Shaun inquired after a moment. 'Are you worried you may lose your job?'

She glanced up at him sharply. 'Why do you ask that?'

'I've got eyes. The Lancasters are a nice old couple, but running the hotel is becoming too much for them,' he said evenly. 'It's sad, but it's a familiar story. Are you afraid you'll lose your job?' he repeated gently.

Laura hesitated, before nodding slowly.

'I've been watching you. You can cope with anything without getting flustered. You're good – so you'll never be out of a job!' Shaun declared emphatically. 'Trust me. I've stayed in dozens of hotels. I know what I'm talking about!'

It was considerate of Shaun to try to cheer her up, Laura thought. But he didn't realise, with all the recent upheaval in her life, her job at Monk's Inn was all she had left to cling to.

'Good luck, James!' Becky dropped her schoolbag and reached up to put her arms about her brother's neck as he sat at the piano in the dining-room. 'I hope you pass!'

'So do I!' James smiled, but he looked pale and anxious. For the past week, his first thought on waking up had been the audition. And all day there had been stomach-churning nervousness. And, last night, he'd scarcely slept at all.

'Here's my lucky shell.' Becky gravely opened her hand to show him a pinkish-orange buckie shell she'd found on the beach three summers ago. 'You can take it with you.'

'I will.' James accepted the token and placed it on top of the piano next to his composition notebook. 'Thank you.'

'Don't forget it!' Becky cautioned, scooping up her bag.

'I won't.' James ruffled her curls. 'Have a good day at school.'

As Becky went out into the hall, Ken turned into the front gate from the beach. Jogging up the cracked stone path, he stamped the sand from his trainers before coming up in to the vestibule.

'Be right with you, Becks.' He hurriedly

pulled on track-suit bottoms over his shorts. 'You get your bike out. I want a word with Jimmy.'

James held his breath, wondering what was coming.

'If I had my way, you wouldn't be going to Manchester today, Jimmy, but...' Ken gave a shrug, extending his hand. 'All the best, son.'

James accepted his father's hand gladly. This was probably the most important day of his life. To take with him his father's good wishes was more than he'd dared hope for.

'Can I borrow your bike again?' Ken queried as an afterthought.

'Sure.' James approved of his father's new interest in exercise and keeping fit. It made sense to take care of your body, especially when you got to Dad's age.

'If you like,' James went on tentatively, not looking at Ken. 'Maybe I could come running with you some morning?'

'That'd be great!' Ken grinned buoyantly. 'I'm already doing more than two miles. I'll soon give you a run for your money!'

After Ken and Becky had gone, James went back to practicing his composition. He had little experience of composing, but playing a piece of his own was part – probably a vital part – of the audition. He was determined to be note perfect.

James was several bars into the soaring, romantic music when he realised he was no longer alone, and stopped playing.

'Sorry. I didn't intend distracting you.' Louise was standing by the couch. 'Shall I leave you alone to go on practicing?'

He grinned ruefully, shaking his head. 'If it's not right by now, it never will be!'

'Music is more than simply technique – it's an expression of emotion.'

Louise came over to stand at his side. 'Before you go into play, try to feel the mood of your music inside yourself. The rest will come naturally.'

'Is that a promise?' he asked dryly.

'You bet!' She laughed.

James, laughed, too. Louise was the only person in the family who had a real passion for music. She understood how much playing and writing meant to him. Just as Mum had understood...

'Your mum would be awfully proud of you today,' Louise murmured, as though reading his thoughts. 'I know I am.'

James gave her an appreciative smile. 'It's a weird feeling. Now it's here at last. It's everything I want. Imagine being able to spend all day, every day, just studying and working and playing music!' he declared enthusiastically. 'If I get in...'

'Concentrate on your music,' Louise advised. 'Put everything else from your mind.'

'Easier said than done!' James responded doubtfully.

The grandfather clock in the hall struck the quarter.

'I'd better go.' James slowly lowered the lid of the piano over the yellowed keys. Going through to the hall, he took his jacket and violin case from the table at the foot of the stairs.

Louise followed him to the front door. 'What time's your train?'

'Not for nearly an hour. I'm meeting Charlotte and walking her to the school bus first.'

'You're sure you have enough money? For lunch and – oh, wait!' Louise darted back indoors, returning in a few seconds. 'Becky's lucky shell!'

'I mustn't forget that!' James smiled, slipping it into his pocket.

'Thanks, Louise.' He hesitated only a fraction before stooping to kiss her cheek. 'For everything. You've been a real friend!'

'You – you're welcome!' she faltered, touched and surprised by his gesture of affection. 'Good luck!'

When the almost empty train pulled into Sandford station that evening, James was relieved there was no-one there to meet him. He felt miserable and disappointed, not ready to face a barrage of questions. Especially not ready to face his father. He wandered aimlessly into the village, unwilling to go home. Finding himself outside Monk's Inn, he realised Laura would still be there working…

'James!' Laura looked up from the desk. 'How–?' The question faded on her lips as she saw her brother's expression. 'I was just about to have a cup of tea,' she began quietly. 'Let's go into my office, shall we?'

As Laura plugged in the electric kettle and popped teabags into the mugs, she purposely didn't press James for explanations.

'I blew it, Laura,' he said eventually. 'It was my one chance – and I blew it.'

Laura's heart sank. 'Do you know that for certain?'

'No – the official decision comes by post. But I'm sure.' James slumped into a chair. The sleeplessness of the previous night and the day's emotions were fast catching up on him. His eyes felt gritty and tired.

'If you haven't had a decision yet, then there's still a chance,' Laura encouraged. 'Isn't there?'

James shook his head. 'When I was sitting waiting to be called I was so nervous I couldn't stop my hands shaking,' he began with some embarrassment. 'Yet, once I started to play, it was just as Louise said it would be. Somehow, I wasn't nervous any more. I even began to think everything was going pretty well. The questions. The interview. All of it, really.'

'That doesn't sound so terrible,' Laura ventured. 'You're not the world's most confident person, Jamie. Perhaps you're being overly pessimistic?'

'If only!' he returned fiercely, suddenly angry at himself. 'I played my composition. When I'd finished, one of the board looked up from his papers and said I'd obviously been heavily influenced by Rachmaninov. It was the way he said it! I knew I'd failed!'

James shrugged defeatedly, saying nothing more. Laura sat silently, watching his expressive face. There was something else, something James wasn't telling her. He drank his tea and got up to leave.

'I made Dad a promise,' he said without turning around. 'I said that, if I didn't get a place, I'd give up music.'

'Oh, no!' Laura knew what that would mean to him.

Brother and sister's eyes met. Neither one spoke, but each was aware exactly what the other was thinking.

'If you won't say it, Laura,' James declared harshly, 'then I might as well. We both know Dad will keep me to my promise!'

A Peace Offering

Although Laura enjoyed her job at Monk's Inn, she'd never liked working on Sundays. Sunday was family day at Spryglass. Church with James and Becky – and Dad, too, when he'd been home on leave. Then Gran and Grandad would come over after the service... Laura and David would savour the only day of the week they could spend together.

But Sundays were different now...

Laura lingered at the hotel as long as she could, before wandering out into the hot sunshine.

She crossed to the green and sat down, but she paid little attention to the cricket match being played.

'Laura!' Shaun Pembridge dropped down on the grass beside her. He was wearing whites, and his face was flushed. 'I spotted you watching while I was playing. That's probably why I was bowled out.' He grinned at her, then lay on his back in the grass. 'Distracted by a pretty girl!'

Laura laughed. It was impossible to take Shaun – or his compliments – too seriously!

'You really should do that more often,' he

observed, running a hand through his fair hair as he turned his head to look up at her. 'It suits you. Why do you always look so sad and lonely, Laura?'

'I don't!' she returned defensively, embarrassed that he should make such a personal remark. 'Do I?'

'You do. Especially when you think there's no-one around to notice,' he said gently, then paused. 'Will you come out with me this evening, Laura? Dancing, perhaps?' His smile was back, his eyes twinkling at her. 'You do like to dance, don't you?'

'Ye-es, I suppose so.' Laura faltered.

David had been her only boyfriend ... she wasn't accustomed to being invited out. Besides, she didn't feel ready to begin seeing somebody else.

'Thanks – but I can't,' she said finally.

'Why not?' Shaun challenged mildly, propping himself on one elbow to study her better.

Laura didn't know how to answer, so said nothing.

'We enjoyed ourselves that afternoon with my niece and her friends, didn't we? Or was I mistaken?'

'Yes – that is, no, you weren't. I did enjoy it.' Laura hesitated, wishing Shaun would stop staring at her that way. It made her uncomfortable. 'But that afternoon was different.'

'How?' he persisted. 'Because the girls were there to chaperone–'

Laura felt the colour rising to her cheeks.

'Forgive me! I shouldn't have teased you!' Shaun touched her hand apologetically. 'I'm too pushy – and I know it!' he added humbly. 'Won't you, at least, have tea with me? I've heard the cricket teas at Monk's are wonderful…'

'They are!' Laura responded to Shaun's smile.

'You'll come with me then?'

'I can't. My family's waiting.'

Laura let herself into Spryglass and went through to the empty kitchen.

Everyone was in the garden. Sunday tea was enjoyed outdoors now, if the weather was fine.

During tea, Nancy observed that almost everything they were eating was home-grown by David at Riverside, or by Dan on his new allotment.

'Ay, it's my first harvest from the plot. Not too bad, is it?' He beamed. 'There'll be plenty of fruit ripe for picking later. That'll come in handy for the barn dance jams and pies.'

The end-of-summer fête and dance at McCobb's barn was to raise funds for the local animal shelter and was eagerly awaited by everyone in Sandford. Laura and Nancy always baked for the occasion.

'Becky's joining in this year!' Laura smiled. 'Her toffee whirls will be sellout!'

'I would like to help, too,' Louise offered. 'If I may?'

'It's thoughtful of you,' Laura replied quickly. 'But Gran and I have everything organised.'

'Oh, I understand,' Louse murmured, glancing along the table. 'More tea, anyone?'

'Yes, please...' Dan replied cheerfully. 'I'm playing the spoons at the barn dance, you know. Now there is something you could do, Louise!' he went on, with a sly look to James. 'Make fancy shirts for James and David – the Singing Cowboys!'

'I was hoping to keep it quiet!' James shrugged sheepishly. 'David and I were working at Riverside, and Mrs Almond came by selling tickets for the barn dance. When David invited her in, she spotted his guitar. Apparently not all the music for the dance was arranged ... and one thing sort of led to another.'

'It sounds fun. I'll be happy to make the shirts, James,' Louise said. 'I'll do a few sketches, and you and David can choose the design you like best.'

'What about you, Laura?' Ken asked. 'You used to be pretty good at sewing. Are you making some fancy outfit for the dance?'

'I'm not going,' Laura answered clearly.

She'd decided that weeks ago. 'I'll be helping at the fête during the afternoon, but in the evening I'll stay at home with Becky.'

'I'm not a baby, Laura!' Becky protested indignantly. 'Besides, I'm going to the barn dance, too!'

'We'll have a nice time at the fête,' Laura said gently. 'But you know you can't go to the dance...'

'Louise said I could!' Becky insisted, turning to her stepmother as she came from the house carrying her sketch pad and colours. 'I can, can't I?'

'Can what?' Louise inquired, sitting next to Ken on the swing.

'Go to the barn dance!'

'Of course, Becky,' she replied, unaware of Laura's disapproving stare. 'We're all going.' Then she sensed the sudden tension. 'Aren't we?'

'It's far too late for Becky,' Laura responded crisply. 'The dance never ends until after midnight.'

'Surely one late night won't hurt?' Louise suggested mildly.

'I want to go, Daddy!' Becky pleaded. 'I can, can't I?'

'We'll all go!' Ken said firmly and Becky threw her arms around his neck in delight. 'It's a late night – but it is the school holidays,' he went on appeasingly. 'And McCobb's barn dance is a family affair, Laura.'

When Grandad persuaded James to fetch his violin and play his cowboy tunes, Laura slipped away to her room. She'd been mother to Becky for so long … it was hard to let go.

She'd been upstairs only a few minutes when James knocked at the door.

'A visitor for you – that Shaun what's-his-name, from Monk's Inn.' James hurriedly looked in from the landing. He was carrying his violin, and two dessert spoons. 'I've put him in the sitting-room.'

Laura went straight down. As Shaun rose to greet her, he proffered a small bouquet of apricot carnations and a large box of chocolates.

'Peace offering,' he said simply. 'I'm sorry if I offended you earlier. Won't you give me another chance? Have dinner with me tonight? Please?'

Laura wavered. For all his brashness, she was discovering that Shaun Pembridge was awfully easy to like. She smiled and agreed to go.

'When you asked if I enjoyed sailing, I didn't guess you had this in mind!' Laura exclaimed.

She and Shaun were standing on the deck of the illuminated paddle-steamer which cruised the river each evening during the summer.

'You haven't been aboard before?' he

inquired. 'Good. I'm glad! And the food's excellent!'

Liverpool and New Brighton were pin-cushions of light in Empress's wake. The open water ahead silver-grey in the glow of the rising moon.

'I've a confession to make...' Shaun spoke softly. 'At least I think I have.'

'Mmm.' Laura wasn't really listening to him.

'Did you know I'm related to the Lan-casters? Beattie is my aunt.'

He had Laura's attention now.

'I wondered why you were staying at Monk's Inn. It never seemed your sort of place somehow.'

'Oh, I don't know. It's quiet and peaceful – just what I needed. I'd had an accident. Needed somewhere to recuperate. Aunt Beattie must have been surprised to get my letter!' he commented. 'She and my father don't get along. I hadn't seen them for years. Don't misunderstand me, my family are wonderful. Dad and Mother have always backed me up – even when I dropped out of university to go off to Spain.' Shaun laughed, shaking his head at the memory. 'That was a real wing-and-a-prayer opera-tion – but I loved every minute!

'I'm a pilot, Laura. Helicopters. Small planes. Gliders. It's my profession – and my passion!' His slim features were animated, his blue-grey eyes alight with enthusiasm. 'I'd rather fly than do anything!'

'Then it was a flying–' Laura began, breaking off in consternation at her tactlessness.

'Yes, it was a flying accident!' he put in brightly, easing her discomfort. 'I mentioned I'd been working in Saudi for several years? I was a pilot for a small air charter company. My plane went down. It wasn't as bad as it sounds, really!' Shaun added quickly, silencing Laura's instinctive concern. 'I was lucky. I'll be flying again in no time. Just need a spot of R and R. I hadn't had a holiday in years, so–' He shrugged, taking Laura's arm as they went into the softly-lit restaurant. 'Here I am!'

Louise tiptoed from the bedroom, not wishing to disturb Ken. Since starting his new teaching job, he hadn't been sleeping well.

'Why didn't you wake me?' Ken demanded in exasperation, striding into the kitchen already shaved and dressed.

'Because you need some sleep!' she returned calmly. 'And besides, you aren't late. There's plenty of time before your train.'

'I wanted to finish grading these papers!' he called through from the sitting-room. His briefcase lay open on a chair, the paperwork he'd brought home spread out across the low table.

'Shall I bring your breakfast in here?'

Louise followed him into the darkly-furnished room.

'Won't have time–' Ken shook his head impatiently.

'Ken – what's wrong?' she murmured. 'If you've got problems...'

'There aren't any problems,' he answered, without looking up from the page he was reading.

'Ken ... each evening, you disappear in here with your work. You hardly sleep at all. You're tense and distant with me ... you snap at the children. Don't shut me out, darling. Tell me what's wrong!'

He glanced at her briefly, gathering the papers together as he did so.

'Don't fuss. There's nothing for you to worry about.' He kissed her forehead. 'See you tonight.'

'Why is Daddy grumpy?' Becky asked out of the blue that day. She and Louise were in the village shopping for buttons for the party dress they were making. 'He never used to be cross all the time.'

'He isn't cross, Becky,' Louise replied sadly. 'He's just working hard at his new job, and he's tired.'

'Oh.' Becky sighed. 'I wish we could do something to cheer him up.'

They left the haberdasher's, and Louise paused to look in the window of the shoe shop.

'School starts again soon. You'll need new shoes,' she remarked. 'You're growing so quickly. I expect you'll need lots of new things.'

'I don't want to go back to school,' Becky murmured, turning away from the window. 'I don't want to go back – ever. I want the holidays to go on for always!'

Louise gave her a cheerful hug. 'There's still the barn dance to look forward to. And your new dress.' She unlocked the car, opening the rear door for Becky. 'And speaking of dresses, do you think we'll be able to help Auntie Helen…?'

'You've done wonders, Louise!' Helen Fairbrass exclaimed, relieved that the cocktail dress which had been unflatteringly tight now fitted smoothly. 'It's an important business dinner, and Alex wanted me to buy something new. But it seemed such a waste when I've a wardrobe full of clothes.' She grimaced, patting her full hips. 'I hadn't realised I'd added a few inches!'

'Can you stay for a coffee and a natter?' she went on as she slipped out of the dress and into slacks and an overshirt. 'Milk and biscuits for you, Becky? Oh, that reminds me! I got a leaflet from the library that'll interest you. It's in the magazine rack in the lounge.'

'This is a lovely house.' Louise looked round at the bungalow's spacious fitted kitchen as her sister-in-law made freshly-ground coffee.

'When we were first married, Alex and I dreamed of living in Ingle Green!' Helen replied wistfully. 'It took us twenty-five years to get here! But sometimes I think we were happier in our little house in Sandford. We were a family then.

'Now, Ashley and Diane are grown up... And Alex doesn't– Oh, just listen to me!' Helen smiled. 'I miss being close to Mum and Dad, and Laura and the children, but...' She shrugged, picking up the tray. 'Let's see if Becky's left us any biscuits!'

They went through to the lounge. Becky lay on her stomach nibbling a biscuit and gazing at a colourful leaflet.

'You're very absorbed!' Louise smiled. 'What are you reading about?'

Becky glanced around quickly. 'Birds.'

'What does it say?' Louise bent to peek over her shoulder.

'It ... it's...' The little girl faltered uncertainly.

'There's a slide show at the Nature Reserve,' Helen supplied, pouring the coffee into mugs. 'I thought Becky might like to go.'

'This looks serious!' James came into the kitchen later that day in search of a snack and found Louise sitting at the table surrounded by cookery books. 'I didn't realise we had any cookery books!'

'Laura doesn't need them!' Louise laughed, then went on more seriously. 'It was something Becky said recently that gave me the idea. Ken has been so ... so...'

'Uptight?'

'Yes,' she agreed soberly. 'I thought perhaps a special dinner might help him unwind. Get the weekend off to a relaxing start.'

'Sounds good. Dad would never let on, but my guess is that he's finding teaching a lot tougher than he expected.' James helped himself to cold pie. 'I promised to take Becky to the slide show at the Nature Reserve next Friday, but we can just as easily go this evening. Laura's working, so it'll give you and Dad some time alone together.'

It had been another long week, and Ken was very relieved it was over at last. He attempted to work on the crowded, noisy train, but finally gave up in exasperation. He put away his books, snapping shut the clasp of his case.

'You're early!' Louise greeted him with obvious pleasure, standing on tiptoe to kiss him. 'What a wonderful surprise. I'm cooking something special, but I'm afraid it won't be ready for a while.'

'That's fine. I've some papers to finish.' Ken held her for a moment.

'I really want us to have this evening, darling,' she whispered. 'Together.'

'Just give me an hour.' He turned into the sitting-room with his briefcase. 'And I'm all yours!'

It was rather more than an hour however, when Ken did finally emerge. Louise brought the meal through to the dining-room and lit the candles.

Afterwards, she curled up next to Ken on the couch. She kissed him, savouring their closeness. 'Oh, I'm so glad it's Friday, darling! This week seemed endless!'

'Don't I know it!' Ken replied with feeling. 'And I've still got a mountain of paperwork to wade through!'

'You're bringing so much work home, you really ought to have a study. After the school holidays are over, could we make a start at redecorating? The girls' bedroom badly needs doing. And the kitchen. But, really, somewhere for you to work is a priority. The sitting-room's fine, but you need a better light. And a proper desk, so you don't have to juggle your papers...'

'Steady on!' Ken interrupted with some amusement. 'I'd like a fancy study ... and to decorate the house from stem to stern! But an old place like this needs constant attention – I never realised how much until I came ashore. We could do with central heating and the window frames could do with renewing. But I've taken such a drop in salary. I don't want any big expenses yet.'

Louise stroked his cheek. 'We can afford it.' She saw his jaw set.

'You mean you can afford it!' he said shortly, moving from her arms. 'I've always provided for my own family. I'm not about to start depending on my wife's money!'

'Don't be so … Victorian!' Louise exclaimed incredulously. 'I can't believe it! We're married, darling. It's our money!'

'It's yours. From the sale of your shop. I'll not touch a penny of it.' He turned to her. 'And you're not to, either. Not for a study, not for the girls' bedroom – not for anything!'

Louise glared at him, her dark eyes glittering with anger. 'How dare you! You're making me feel like an outsider! This is my family now! Spryglass is my home! You're just being stubborn and unreasonable. And selfish–'

'That's enough! I've made up my mind!' With that Ken got up and left the room.

Louise sat alone in the candlelight. She was trembling, her anger spent. The evening which started so hopefully had ended in their first row.

She blew out the candles and cleared the dishes. She regretted losing her temper – but Ken just didn't realise how much he'd hurt her!

David Hale came up from the shore and looked into the garden, where Louise was cutting roses.

'Is James about?'

'I heard music from his room a while ago.' She smiled. 'Go on up.'

A few seconds later, David came downstairs again.

'James isn't there.' He ginned. 'Guess I'll have to catch up with my pardner later!'

That evening, when Ken was working, Louise started hand-sewing multi-coloured sequins and glass beads on to the fringed yokes and shoulders of the shirts she was making for the boys.

At dusk, she called Becky indoors and put her to bed. James still wasn't back. A couple of hours later, when Laura came home from Monk's Inn, Louise asked if James had mentioned going out somewhere.

Laura shook her head. 'He's probably with Charlotte,' she suggested. 'Or at McCobb's barn?'

'Would you like something to eat?' Louise asked absently, her thoughts with James.

'No, thanks.' Laura stifled a yawn, staring upstairs. 'All I want tonight is a bath and bed!'

Louise hovered in the hall, looking at the rod of light shining from beneath the door of the sitting-room. Ken was still engrossed

117

in his work.

Throwing a sweater around her shoulders, she went to the garden shed. James' bicycle was missing. Back inside, she discovered his house-keys on the hall table. Then, for no reason she could explain, Louise checked the fridge and the pantry. Wherever he'd gone, James had taken food with him!

Louise didn't wait another second before rushing to Ken and pouring out her fears.

'I'm sure you're fretting over nothing,' he said calmly. 'Jimmy is often out later than this. He's probably with his pals and lost track of time. Lads his age do that sort of thing. You're surely not imagining he's run off?'

Ken intended this remark lightly, but Louise took it absolutely seriously.

'James is far too considerate to do such a thing. But he's troubled and unhappy – and he's been gone hours… I'm taking the car to drive around and look for him!'

'Louise! I'll go!' He strode after her, grabbing his coat from the rack. 'You can't go roaming–' The telephone shrilled as Ken was on the doorstep.

'Dad?'

'Jimmy!' Ken's voice was unintentionally sharp. 'Are you all right?'

'Yes. I–'

'Wait a minute–' Ken put down the phone, running to the open doorway. 'Louise!' he shouted above the noise of the starting engine. 'Jimmy – he's OK!'

'I went for a ride to get my head together.' James explained over the crackly line when Ken picked up the receiver again. 'I went farther than I realised. Then I got a puncture miles from anywhere. I couldn't fix it, so I had to walk for hours before I even came to a phone box.'

'Have you any idea what time it is?' Ken rubbed the palm of his hand roughly over his forehead. 'And where exactly are you, Jimmy?'

'Somewhere near Rufford Hall.'

'Rufford? That's miles away! Of all the irresponsible–'

'I'm sorry if you were worried, Dad,' James chipped in apologetically.

'I wasn't–' Ken broke off as he heard Louise coming into the hall. Sensing her standing beside him, he reached for her, pulling her close. He was grateful for the warmth of her against him. Grateful that Jimmy was safe. 'I was worried, Jimmy … and scared,' Ken murmured, his tone uncharacteristically soft. He hesitated, bending to touch his lips to Louise's raised face. Her eyes were glistening with tears.

'It was great seeing your car coming towards me the other night!' James confessed as he and Ken jogged along the hard sand fringing the pine woods. 'I was about ready to sleep under a hedge!'

'Would've served you right!' Ken said breathlessly. 'I was all for leaving you – but Louise insisted we went to fetch you.'

They reached the lifeboat station, and turned around for home.

Becky had been up with the lark, and was already wearing her new party dress when James and then Ken burst into the kitchen.

'We raced from the beach,' Ken puffed, clutching the sink. 'I let the lad win–'

'Naturally.' Louise pushed a glass of orange juice into his hands.

'Wow! Who's this pretty girl!' James exclaimed, as Becky appeared from the pantry, carefully carrying the toffee whirls she'd made. 'Have you got a date for the barn dance tonight, Becky? Or am I in with a chance?'

Becky's reply was drowned out by Smokey's barking. Dog and child raced to the front door to retrieve the post.

'One for Laura, and one for you, James!'

James' smile faded. Unceremoniously, he tore open the envelope.

'They've offered me a place,' James' face broke into an astonished beam. 'I'm going to music college!'

The kitchen erupted into voices and questions and barking. Becky flung her arms about James' waist. Louise hugged him hard. Ken hesitated only a second before thumping his son's shoulder.

'Well done, Jimmy! I'm proud of you!'

Presently, James went upstairs to shower and change for his milk round. He met Laura on the landing. She was on her way to work, too.

'Becky's just told me your news!' she exclaimed, kissing his cheek. 'I'm so happy for you, Jamie!'

'Thanks. Oh, this is for you!' He handed Laura her letter. 'Who's it from?'

'Shaun.' She slipped it unopened into her pocket.

'Shaun Pembridge?' James echoed in surprise. 'You see him every day at Monk's Inn!'

'He's been in Staffordshire visiting his family,' Laura explained, checking her handbag. 'But he'll be back in time for the barn dance.'

'You're not starting to go out with him, Laura?' James exclaimed abruptly. 'What about David?'

'David ended our relationship – not me.' Laura's quiet voice was dangerously close to anger. 'I'm free to see whoever I choose.'

She turned away from him, running lightly down the narrow staircase.

'And it's none of your business!'

'David Confided In You?'

It had been the happiest day of James' life. Getting a place at college and playing at the barn dance. Charlotte, and the whole family, pleased and proud of him...

James re-lived every wonderful, special, minute of it as he ambled through the village after walking Charlotte home.

Approaching the Jessups' flat, he saw that their lights were still on. James smiled. Grandad had been a big hit with his spoons, and Gran had won a prize for guessing the weight of a cake. He rang the bell, then had to wait a while for an answer.

'James! Come on in!' Nancy was tying the cord of her dressing-gown. 'Sorry to keep you on the doorstep. I was getting ready for bed!

'Dan mustn't have heard the bell.' She smiled as they went indoors. 'He's making cocoa–' She broke off, her hand flying to her throat as she pushed open the kitchen door. 'Dan!'

James moved quickly past her and fell to his knees on the linoleum. Dan lay pale and still. Taking his grandfather's wrist, James fumbled for a pulse-beat. If there was one, he couldn't feel it. Every split second was vital. James had never felt so scared or helpless or clumsy or slow as he heaved at his grandfather's inert body, turning him on to his back.

'Get an ambulance, Gran. Quick–' He bent Dan's head full back ... then, with thumb and forefinger, pinched his nose closed.

James' own chest was so tight he could scarcely take the deep breath necessary as he lowered his face to Dan's. Exhaling. Inhaling. Counting. He had to give these first four breaths very fast–

James had taken classes with the St John's years ago. Ken had insisted he learned first aid before he'd take him out sailing. Now he forced his agitated brain to remember, praying he was doing it right.

Third breath. Watching Grandad's chest rise and fall. Fourth breath... If after this one there was no pulse...

'Got it!' he yelled at the top of his voice. The pulse was weak, but it was there.

'Oh ... thank heaven...' James heard Gran's slippered feet coming behind him into the kitchen. Her hand touched his hair. 'The ambulance is on its way.' Nancy could hardly speak. 'Oh, Jamie – if you hadn't been here...'

James darted a sidelong glance up at her. The look in her eyes was the saddest thing he'd ever seen. He sent her upstairs to get dressed.

Was this it, she agonized. Was she going to lose him? He'd been ill before. But this time was different. This time, it had happened so suddenly. Swift footsteps in the hall. Loud voices. James' shout of relief. Suddenly everything was happening in an unreal blur of noise and speed and activity.

James had been waiting for the opportunity to find a pay phone and call Dad and Louise, but he didn't want to leave Gran on her own just yet. They were sitting in the quietness of a waiting area just along the corridor from the Intensive Care Unit, where Grandad had been rushed by the ambulancewoman and waiting nurses.

'There's a machine over there,' he said. 'I'll get you some tea. They've got biscuits and snacks, too. Would you like anything?'

'Just tea.' Nancy smiled up at him.

James crossed to the vending machine, slotting in the coins. His reflection stared back at him from the machine's mirrored panel. He was still wearing the brightly-sequinned cowboy shirt. The barn dance, all the fun and laughter... It seemed so far away. The family had been so happy. Grandad singing along, joking, full of life and smiling... Now the whole world was upside down. Just like it was when they lost Mum...

James took the strong tea to Nancy, wrapping the scalding-hot plastic cup in his handkerchief before handing it to her. 'Army tea!' she declared, taking a small sip. 'That's what Grandad would call this!'

'So strong you could dye your boots with it!' James finished with a wan smile. 'Gran – will you be OK while I find a phone and call home?'

The phone at Spryglass seemed to ring forever before finally someone answered. It was Ken who came to the phone. James quickly explained.

'I'll come straight away,' Ken said tersely. 'Oh, Jimmy! Does Helen know?'

'Auntie Helen – I'd forgotten about her!' James muttered in dismay. 'As soon as I put down the phone, I'll call her.'

'No, don't call her. Alex is still away at some toy show or other so, unless Ashley or Diane are home for the weekend, Helen will be on her own. I don't want her hearing bad news like this over the phone, then driving all the way to the hospital,' Ken concluded, as Louise came silently downstairs.

'I'll go over to Ingle Green, and we'll come in together.' He paused. 'Is Laura with you?'

'No. Isn't she home yet?' James was surprised. He'd noticed Laura leaving the dancing with Shaun Pembridge, but that had been hours before the end. 'She doesn't usually stay out this late!'

'True – but, as I keep reminding myself, Laura's a grown woman with a life of her own. And this Shaun seems a decent enough lad,' Ken remarked with a resigned sigh. 'Give our love to Gran, Jimmy. And tell her we'll get there as soon as we can.'

After leaving the dance, Shaun and Laura had driven out to Beacon Point. There, the dunes were so high, she felt she could reach out and touch the tops of the tall, ragged pines that fringed the beach below. It was strangely disturbing to discover just how much she wanted to stay in Shaun's arms.

Shaun bent to kiss Laura's forehead.

Laura moved slightly in his arms, and he held her closer. She'd already become very special to him. When he'd arrived in Sandford, he'd never expected fortune to turn in his favour once more. But it had. He'd met Laura. She was warm and sweet and, although it was in Shaun's nature to be impetuous, for once in his life, he'd had sense enough not to rush. He didn't want to frighten her.

Laura wasn't like other girls he'd known. She was reserved, wary of being hurt. Shaun had heard local gossip about her broken relationship with David Hale, and he'd taken pains to win her confidence and, hopefully, to gain her trust. He opened his eyes, gazing down at her face in the cool, blue light of morning. She was lovely. That sundress with the scallopy-bits on the straps looked great and it was typically modest. So like Laura…

'Laura, I want us to go away somewhere together,' Shaun said impulsively, his sensible intentions swept away. 'Will you come with me?'

She turned around in his arms, raising her face to his, and he resisted the urge to kiss her. 'Oh, Shaun … I can't!' she murmured.

'Why not?' he asked quietly.

'It's not that I don't care for you,' she answered guilelessly. 'I do. Very much. It's just that we haven't really known each other for long and–'

'Shhh, it's OK. Don't look so worried!' Shaun pulled her tight against him, shaken by the jolt of excitement rushing through him. 'Patience isn't one of my virtues. I probably don't even have any virtues–' he murmured thickly. 'But I do understand. Honestly, I do…'

Laura could only whisper his name as he moved closer.

Shaun was only the second man ever to really kiss her. And she felt breathless and overwhelmed by the strength of emotion flowing between them. She didn't want the moment to end.

'…I suppose I'd better take you home,' he murmured at last, unwillingly releasing her from his embrace. 'Or I'll never want to take you home again!'

Shaun drove slowly, reaching Spryglass all too soon. They said a lingering, reluctant goodbye, and Laura watched until his car disappeared from sight along the sand-dusted crescent. Then she went quickly into the silent house.

It was Sunday and still early. Laura slipped off her shoes and ran lightly up the stairs, opening the door into the attic bedroom noiselessly so as not to awaken Becky.

Then she stopped. The covers of Becky's bed were rumpled, but her sister wasn't there.

Had she slipped out into the garden to feed her birds? Laura started downstairs again.

Passing James' room, she glanced through the open door. The bed obviously hadn't been slept in.

What on earth had happened?

Where was everybody–?

'Laura!'

She half turned to see Louise emerging, barefoot, on to the landing. Looking past her into the room, Laura could see Becky curled up in the big double bed, sleeping soundly.

But Dad wasn't there.

'What's going on?' Laura began, her alarmed voice sounding loud in the quietness of the old house.

Louise raised a finger to her lips, partially closing the bedroom door so as not to disturb Becky.

'I'm sorry – I must have fallen asleep,' she whispered. 'I intended waiting up for you. Your grandfather's been taken ill,' she said gently, her hand reaching out to touch the younger woman's arm. 'Ken and James have been at the hospital all night.'

It was a warm, sunny September afternoon, a blackberrying afternoon, Grandad would've called it. He loved ambling along the country lanes with his grandchildren, spinning his tall tales and picking ripe berries for Gran to make into his favourite jam.

Gran had suggested the outing. Laura and James had collected Becky from school and now they strolled along together, while their young sister dawdled, sampling as many berries as she collected, and spotting the hedgerow butterflies and birds.

'All the doctors ever seem to say is that he's "Very poorly but stable",' James commented despairingly. 'What does that mean?'

Laura sighed. She understood James' anxiety. The whole family was desperate for some hopeful news.

'When he opens his eyes, and we hold his hand, do you think he really knows we're there?' James went on unhappily.

'I'm sure he does,' she answered with conviction.

Grandad was drifting in and out of deep sleep. Whenever he stirred, there was someone there, so he'd hear a comforting voice, see a familiar face.

'I'm not keen on leaving for college,' James said, when they were taking a short-cut through the pinewoods towards the allotments. 'Not with Grandad the way he is.'

'Gran'll have something to say if you don't go!' Laura smiled, pausing while Becky set out blackberries on a tree stump for the bright-eyed squirrels watching from high in the pines. 'And Grandad will, too, when – when he gets better,' she added firmly.

'Do you truly think–' James began, but Laura interrupted him.

'There's David! What's he doing at Grandad's allotment?' she exclaimed sharply, as the neat plots of flowers, fruit and vegetables came into sight through the thinning trees.

James shrugged. 'We've both been looking after it.'

Laura wheeled to face him. 'Did you know David would be here?'

'Don't be silly!' he returned shortly. 'It was your idea to pick some of Grandad's flowers for him! Besides, there would be no point in trying to get you together with David. You've made it perfectly plain you don't care about him any more!'

'That's a dreadful thing to say!' Laura retorted, more hurt than annoyed. 'I do care about David. I always shall!'

'You certainly haven't shown it lately!' James countered abruptly. 'David doesn't have any family of his own – none that he's close to, at any rate. And you know how much Grandad means to him. He's as scared and worried as the rest of us, yet you haven't once been out to Riverside, or even phoned him! Just because you're going out with Shaun Pembridge isn't any excuse to treat David so … cruelly!'

Laura stared, shocked by her mild-mannered brother's angry outburst. Had she really been so insensitive and selfish? Laura's honest, inward answer filled her with remorse and left her unable to reply.

'For all his smooth talk and flashy ways, Shaun Pembridge doesn't have any genuine feelings for you!' James finished emphatically. 'If he did, he wouldn't have left you alone and taken off to London just when you needed him most!'

'Shaun had to go to London!' Laura retaliated defensively. 'It was something to do with his work. I don't know what–'

James shook his head impatiently. 'Why can't you see him for what he really is?' he demanded. 'All Shaun cares about is Shaun! He'll let you down!'

'Stop it, James!' Laura warned, her temper

rising. 'You don't know what you're talking about. You don't even know Shaun!'

James glared at her, his gentle eyes blazing. 'Do you?' he challenged.

The autumn afternoons were drawing in quite early now. It was already dusk, but Louise and Becky were still busy tidying the back garden.

'I love sweeping leaves. Grandad made me this witch's broom 'specially,' Becky explained, pausing red-cheeked and breathless with the child-sized besom clutched in both hands. 'Should we leave some leaves for Daddy to sweep?'

'Oh, he'd like that!' Louise laughed, loading the barrow. She turned at the sound of a motorcycle approaching the front of the house. 'That's Shaun bringing Laura home. I hadn't realised it was that time already!' She started indoors. 'I haven't even thought about a meal yet!'

But when Louise reached the kitchen she realised the last thing on Laura's mind was food.

'What gorgeous flowers!' Louise exclaimed. 'From Shaun?'

Laura nodded happily, the faintest blush coming to her cheeks.

'He left them on my desk this morning.'

'Oh, if only Ken were so romantic!' Louise laughed gently. 'I can't remember when he last gave me flowers. Or Belgian chocolates!'

'I don't think Dad's the flowers and chocs type, somehow!' Laura smiled self-consciously.

They both laughed this time and Louise fetched the fresh vegetables from the pantry.

'Louise—' Laura began uncertainly, when they were scrubbing the veg. 'I'd like to ask David to dinner.'

'That's a good idea,' Louise replied evenly, concealing her surprise. Up till now Laura had gone to considerable lengths to avoid David Hale.

'How abut Thursday?' Louise suggested.

'No – not then. Shaun is having to go to London again,' Laura said awkwardly. 'If David comes to dinner, it'll seem ... well, that while Shaun's away I'm—'

'I understand,' Louise responded tactfully. 'So when are you inviting David?'

'I'm not!' Laura looked at her in consternation. 'That is, I thought... Would you ask him?'

'I believe the invitation would mean a great deal more to David,' Louise replied in a measured tone, 'if it came from you. He's feeling very down at the moment. Worried about Dan, of course, but there's more to it than that. The casual gardening work David's done through the summer has come to an end now. He's having to rely entirely on the market garden. The winter months

133

will be very difficult.'

'You've seen him?' Laura inquired casually.

'Oh, yes. He brings me things from Dan's allotment. And I've been out to Riverside on several occasions.'

'And David confided in you?' Laura's eyes remained lowered, but her voice was unexpectedly sharp.

'We've talked, yes.' Louise frowned. 'Remember, I've also struggled to make a small business survive. I can understand what he's going through. If you ask him to dinner with the family David would be very pleased.'

Laura didn't comment. She finished chopping the carrots, dried her hands, and went through to set the table.

Nancy's telephone call from the hospital came just as Louise and Becky arrived home from school. Seconds later, they were driving into the village.

At Monk's Inn, Becky raced from the car, through the lobby and into Laura's office. 'Grandad's better!' she shouted, flinging herself at her sister. 'Grandad's better!'

Laura's astonished eyes met Louise's above her head.

'Dan's being transferred into an ordinary ward!' Louise explained.

Laura took a deep, thankful breath. She realised there was still a long way to go before Grandad would be well again. But, at least, the worst was over. Suddenly she felt weak at the knees and sank down into her chair.

'Louise said we could go to see Grandad tonight!' Becky told her excitedly.

'I hoped we might all visit the hospital together,' Louise ventured. She wanted Laura's approval for what would surely be a tremendously emotional family gathering. 'What do you think?'

'It's a wonderful idea.' Laura responded with genuine pleasure. 'Grandad will be delighted to see the whole family! Well, except for Jamie. What a pity he won't be here.'

'I can drive to Manchester and bring him back,' Louise began enthusiastically. 'He doesn't know about Dan yet. Nor do Ken and David. I'll telephone when we get home.'

'Why not phone from here?' Laura suggested, getting up from her desk and smiling from Louise to Becky. 'And while she's doing it, why don't we go in to the kitchen and choose the best cake we can find to take home for tea?'

A few minutes later Becky gazed at the chilled glass shelves of gateaux, pavlovas and cheesecakes. She was spoilt for choice.

Laura spun around as the outer door was pulled open, banging back loudly against the catch.

'Shaun!' She was thrilled to see him. 'I didn't expect you back–'

'I didn't expect to be back,' he returned tersely, pushing a hand through his hair as he strode across the kitchen. 'I need to talk to you.'

'I'm at work!' she began to protest, then her heart lurched as she saw the distress in his eyes. 'I'll be finished in about twenty minutes,' she said more gently. 'We'll talk then.'

'This won't wait.' He grasped her wrist urgently. 'It's important. I must see you. Alone. Please!'

Shaun impatiently paced the floor of his room at Monk's Inn. He threw himself down on the seat by the window and stared out despairingly at the village shops with their illuminated windows. A second later, and he was on his feet again. Pacing. Pacing. Where was Laura?

Shaun bit his lip. All those months of treatment, physio, counselling... He'd gone through it all for nothing!

There was a quiet tap at the door. Laura came in carrying a tray of coffee and sandwiches. 'I thought you'd want something to–' she began softly, settling down the tray. 'Why are you in the dark? And it's freezing in here! I'll close the curtains and–'

'Leave the curtains!' He caught her in his arms and held her fiercely. His voice was muffled and indistinct as he bent to kiss her.

'Shaun, what happened?' Laura whispered fearfully.

He pulled away from her. Too agitated, too distraught to be still.

'What I told you about my accident,' he began at last. 'It was true – but selective. It wasn't exactly the harmless little prang I implied. It was serious.' He sank on to the window seat, gazing up at her. 'Pretty grim in fact. I was hospitalised overseas, then they flew me back to the UK for further surgery and treatment.'

'You were badly hurt?' she cried in alarm. 'But you said–'

Shaun sighed and sank down on the window seat. 'When the doctors told me the chances of my ever being fit enough to fly again were remote, I refused to believe them,' he answered simply. 'I came to Sandford determined to prove them wrong. I nearly did it, too!'

The sadness of his smile tore at Laura's heart. Impulsively, she wrapped her arms around him, allowing herself to be drawn down on to his lap.

'You're sweet, Laura...' Shaun sighed, snuggling her to him. 'I never wanted to have to tell you ... but I've been going to London to see just about every consultant, specialist and clinic in the book.' He smiled bleakly.

'I came to the end of my list this afternoon. They all said the same thing. I'm as fit as I'll ever be – but no more flying.' There was no smile now, to conceal the bitterness behind the words. 'Flying was all I lived for!'

There was a charged, tense silence.

'You've had a dreadful disappointment,' Laura ventured at last. 'But you're alive and well. Life has many–'

'Don't tell me to count my blessings!' he cut in warningly.

'That's exactly what I'm asking you to do,' Laura murmured gently. 'It's all any of us can do when we're in trouble. That, and practical things to help.' She moved quietly around the room, closing the curtains, switching on the lamps and the log-fire, so that warmth and light replaced the chill darkness. 'This coffee's cold.' She gave him a small smile. 'And you look the same. I'll send up some more – and some supper on a tray. This time, don't waste it!'

'You're not going back to work?' he exclaimed in disbelief.

'I have to,' she replied mildly. 'Since the Lancasters let the full-time staff go, there's only Ruby and me. We've got a golden anniversary dinner party booked in this evening and–'

'There's always something with you, Laura!' Shaun snapped vehemently. 'If it's not your family, it's your job. Never once do

138

I come first in your priorities!'

'It isn't that way at all!' Laura protested, touching his face. 'You mean far more to me than you realise. But I do have responsibilities – people who depend upon me. I can't let them down.'

'Then I'll see you when you finish work?' he said, still annoyed.

'No,' she replied gently. 'My family and I are going to the hospital. Grandad came out of intensive care today.'

'OK.' Shaun gave a brief, grudging nod of acceptance as Laura took the tray and left the room.

A Difference Of Opinion

The evening Ken set off for a week-long college field trip, Louise put Becky to bed and slipped the storybook they were reading under the pillow. The little girl's reading was progressing well, since Louise had been spending extra time helping her.

Louise kissed Becky good-night again, and went down to press the gingham jam pot covers they'd made together. Spryglass had never seemed so large and empty. The grandfather clock in the hall seemed to tick louder than ever as she smoothed the iron over Becky's neat cross-stitching.

This was foolish! Ken had been gone only a few hours. How could she be pining for him already?

It was raining heavily next morning. Laura came downstairs shortly after Louise. The two women hardly spoke. It wasn't because they'd fallen out. In fact, Louise was delighted at how well she was getting on with Ken's elder daughter now. But they still weren't close enough for Laura to confide in her. And Louise could guess at the reason for her stepdaughter's recent moodiness – Shaun Pembridge!

Laura was in the hall fetching her raincoat when Becky squeezed by, still in her nightie and slippers, and went into the kitchen.

'Becky! Why aren't you dressed yet?' Louise smiled at her from the stove. 'We'll be late for school if you don't hurry!'

'I don't feel well.' Louise knelt down and took both of Becky's hands. They were ice-cold and clammy, and her face was drained of colour. 'You're awfully cold. Come over beside the fire,' she suggested gently. 'Perhaps you'll feel better after you've eaten your breakfast.'

'Don't want it,' she murmured forlornly.

'Becky – where does it hurt?' Laura asked, kindly but firmly. She'd come into the kitchen, and now touched her sister's forehead and looked into her face. 'Where don't you feel well?'

Becky looked away from Laura. 'All over.'

'Away you go and eat your breakfast.' Laura smiled sympathetically and gave her a hug. 'Then get ready for school.'

'I don't want to go to school!' Becky tugged away from her and darted across the kitchen to Louise. 'I feel sick. I want to stay at home!'

'Suppose I take you to school today?' Laura said brightly. 'Once you get there, you'll be all right.'

'I want to stay here!' Becky sobbed, her blue eyes huge.

Louise felt Becky's cold hand slip into hers.

She was relieved that the child wasn't actually ill, but, just the same, Becky was genuinely distressed.

She looked so small and alone and unhappy.

'Becky, go upstairs and get dressed. Then we'll have breakfast.' Louise was unsure, even as she spoke, that she was acting wisely. 'You can stay at home today.'

The little girl didn't need any second bidding.

'Why did you do that?' Laura demanded shortly, as she fled up the stairs. 'You know there's nothing wrong with her!'

'I'm keeping Becky at home today,' Louise replied evenly. 'Because this is where she wants to be. Badly.'

Laura shook her head in exasperation. 'You should have backed me up, not encouraged her,' she said tersely, buttoning her raincoat. 'If Dad were here, he'd agree.'

'Ken isn't here!' Louise returned crisply. 'While I may not be Becky's mother, I regard her as my daughter. And I'll do whatever I believe to be in her best interests.'

Laura took a quick, sharp breath.

'As you say, you're responsible for Becky now.' She tied the belt of her raincoat tightly and picked up her bag from the dresser. 'But you're wrong to let her miss school!'

'Becky won't tell me what's wrong, Dan,' Louise said anxiously later that morning, while Becky was temporarily out of hearing. 'I shouldn't have kept her from school. Laura was right. I should have listened to her.'

'Hmmm, happen you were both a bit right. And a bit wrong!' Dan replied mildly. 'Would you like me to try to find out what's bothering her?'

'I'd be grateful. Otherwise, I won't know how to begin to help her—' She broke off, as Becky was coming into the hospital day-room where Dan now spent much of his time.

'Hello, darling,' Louise began, getting up from the chair next to Dan's. 'I'm just popping along to – to–'

'The hospital shop,' Dan chipped in helpfully, craning his neck to peep into the small basket Becky was carrying. 'What have you got there, Becky?'

'It's for you!' She smiled, swishing away a tea-towel to reveal a dumpy glass jar topped with an embroidered lid cover. 'James and Laura and me went blackberrying. Then Gran and me made the jam, and Louise showed me how to do the little cover!'

'My favourite jam, eh?' Dan chuckled.

'Will you be coming home soon?' Becky clambered on to his knees.

'I hope so – hospital food isn't a patch on Gran's cooking.' He lowered his voice. 'The rice pudding looks like something you'd stick wallpaper on with!'

'It's like that at school!' Becky laughed.

'Why didn't you want to go today?' Dan asked amiably.

'I've been picked to read a poem in the Christmas play,' she answered matter-of-factly, folding the tea-towel neatly. 'We were going into the hall to practise today. Mr Carruthers told me I'd have to stand up on the stage and read out of a book.' She hesitated, looking away and fiddling with the corner of the tea-towel.

'And?' Dan prompted, giving her a gentle nudge.

'I was scared, Grandad.'

'Phew! Tricky, isn't it?' Dan remarked, scratching his chin thoughtfully. 'You know those cassette tapes I've been getting since I've been in here?'

Becky nodded. He'd let her put on the headphones and listen to bits of the stories.

'Well, I've got an idea...'

'So how's it coming along?' Helen asked cheerfully when she and Louise were shopping in the village.

Louise had just stocked up on scarlet and holly-green crêpe paper, packets of sticky-glitter and gold doilies.

'Marvellously! It's tremendous fun!' she responded enthusiastically. Along with several other parents she and Ken had volunteered to help make costumes and scenery for Becky's school play. 'The girls are all delighted to be fairies and sugar plums – but the boys aren't too keen to be dressed up as candy cones and pumpkins!'

'I can imagine the difficulties!' Helen laughed, as they turned into the haberdasher's before going on to meet Ken and Becky at the library. 'Oh, I envy you, Louise. I loved it when Ashley and Diane were little and we did things together!'

'It is fun,' Louise agreed warmly. 'Especially watching Becky enjoy herself. She was awfully nervous at first – convinced she'd never be able to read aloud. But Dan's idea of her speaking into his cassette recorder, and then playing it back so she could actually hear herself reading, gave her the confidence she lacked.'

'I wondered what Dad was up to!' Helen exclaimed with a smile. 'I asked, but he wouldn't say!'

'Becky probably swore him to secrecy!' Louise replied, selecting several rolls of shiny ribbon and moving along to the trays of buttons. 'She likes secrets! What do you think, Helen?' She held several glittering, crystal-effect buttons on her palm. 'Sparkly enough for a snowman?'

'Definitely! But isn't it about time you began thinking of this sort of thing?' Helen jokingly indicated a display of fine, super-soft, white yarn. 'It would knit up into a beautiful layette...'

'I'm sure it would!' Louise laughed, choosing the glass buttons. 'But, when we got married, Ken and I had agreed not to have a family.'

'Ah, I see.' Helen nodded. She could understand her brother-in-law's decision not to have more children at his age. But she'd watched Louise and Becky together ... seen the tenderness in Louise's eyes when she spoke of the child.

Helen couldn't help wondering how much longer she would be content to abide by that decision.

Laura sat before the dressing-table mirror teasing a comb through her damp hair. It had been a bitterly cold, dreary day and she'd been glad to leave Monk's Inn and come home. She hadn't seen Shaun all day.

He'd driven off after supper last night, so Mrs Lancaster explained. He hadn't said where he was going, nor when he'd be back. And he hadn't left a message for Laura.

She sighed, putting down the comb and staring despondently at her reflection in the mirror. Shaun had been depressed these past weeks. Laura had tried to be with him as much as she could, tried to help him... She understood the reasons for his caustic moods and made allowances for them.

In so many ways, he was still a complete mystery to her. His attitudes, the things he did – she'd never in her life met anyone quite like him. Sometimes, she felt she hardly even knew him. Then there were days when she didn't see him – they felt endless, and un-bearably empty.

Feeling suddenly cold, Laura went down-stairs to the warm, brightly-lit living-room. She sat by the fire, toasting her toes on the hearth as her father, Becky and Louise hurried back and forth pulling on warm coats and scarves. They were taking the ferry across the water to Wallasey, having tea out, and then going on to the cinema.

Ken paused in the doorway and glanced back at her questioningly.

Laura smiled cheerfully, and shook her head decisively.

'I really have got things to do, Dad!'

She'd hardly taken up her pad and pen when there was an impatient thud on the front door's heavy brass knocker.

Before they'd exchanged a word, Shaun exuberantly kissed Laura's lips, sponta-neously banishing the weeks of coolness and distance. She responded instinctively, their re-established intimacy both pleasurable and wonderfully reassuring.

'I met your family at the corner. Your

father said you needed cheering up, and you'd be pleased to see me.' Shaun looked down, studying her with twinkling eyes.

Laura was vexed to feel herself blushing. Why did Dad say such things?

'Are you pleased?' Shaun persisted mischievously, brushing her flushed cheek with his lips.

'As if you need to ask!' she owned up shyly.

'Don't be embarrassed!' Shaun's voice was suddenly tender. 'It's the same for me. When I'm away from you, all I can think about is this ... the moment when I'll get back to you.' He held her close.

'It was thinking about you that turned today around for me,' he continued at last, slipping an arm about her as they started into the fire-lit living-room. 'You know I've received the insurance and compensation for my accident? Well, I had to go to London to tie up a last few loose ends.

'It was ghastly. Like a funeral. Everything that's been going on in my head these last weeks just crowded in on me. From having a career I loved, a life I loved, suddenly I had nothing. No present. No future. No hope left...' Shaun's voice trailed off, and he shrugged, shame-faced. 'What I was doing – what I've been doing – is wallowing in self-pity.

'Then I came up from the Tube at Covent

Garden and there was a street flower-seller near the opera house. I wasn't even looking, but I saw this...' From his jacket pocket, Shaun withdrew a rosebud and offered it to Laura.

'Oh, Shaun...' she murmured, touched by the simple gift. The flower was rather faded and crushed, but the biggest bouquet in the world couldn't have meant more to her at that moment.

'I don't know how you've put up with me recently,' Shaun said quietly. 'I saw those flowers and started thinking about you ... and for the first time since the accident, instead of looking back, I began looking ahead. The past is over. It's time for me to move on–'

'You're not going away?' Laura breathed, her eyes revealing all she was feeling. 'Leaving Sandford?'

'How could I? When you're here?' he asked softly. 'No – I'm staying. I'm going to buy Monk's Inn.'

'Buy Monk's?' Laura echoed in astonishment.

Shaun had always been critical of the little hotel with its homely atmosphere.

'Oh, it's run-down at the moment,' he went on. 'But that's only because it has become far too much for Frank and Beattie to cope with. But there's no denying it's got charm and character. And potential!' he added enthusiastically. 'About four years ago, an old friend from university bought a sixteenth-century tavern not far from Stratford-upon-Avon. It was virtually in ruins when Miles got his hands on it, but he's restored it and now it's the most gorgeous, romantic little country hotel you've ever set eyes on.

'I'd like to take you there sometime,' he added almost hesitantly, remembering her previous rejections. 'Would you come?'

'Yes,' Laura answered quietly, her earlier reservations dispelled. 'Yes, I think I would, Shaun.'

'Super!' For once he was almost lost for words. 'Great!' He smiled at her in delight. 'I'll get on to Miles and make some arrangements. You'll love the Hearts of Oak. It's an ... enchanting ... place. And I use that word deliberately! It's got just the sort of look ... feel ... I want Monk's Inn to have. I may not know as much about Shakespeare and antiques as Miles Weaver, but what he's done with the Hearts, I can do with Monk's Inn!'

'What do Mr and Mrs Lancaster think of it all?' Laura asked suddenly. It was difficult to imagine Monk's without the elderly couple! 'I bet they were nearly as surprised as me!'

'They don't actually know yet.' Shaun grimaced. 'I wanted to tell you first.'

'Oh!'

'Exactly.' He sighed soberly. 'Monk's is rapidly going downhill, but I'm not sure Frank and Beattie will be keen to sell. What do you think?'

'I don't know. And it isn't for me to say.' Laura was very conscious of her loyalty to the elderly couple. 'The Lancasters are more than my employers, they're friends. It doesn't feel right, even to be discussing them this way. All I can really tell you is what you already know. The inn has been their home for years, and they care about it.'

'I was afraid you'd say something like that,' Shaun admitted despondently. 'I know I'm related to them, but you know them far better than I do. They respect and value your judgement. If you dropped a few comments about the wisdom of selling up before the place deteriorates any further, I'm sure they'd listen. Then when I app-roach them with my offer, they'll already be softened-up–'

Laura stared at him in total disbelief. 'Shaun, that's deceitful!' she exclaimed, disappointed he'd even asked her. Hurt and offended that he'd imagined her capable of such a thing.

'It's business, Laura!' he reasoned patiently.

'Well, it certainly isn't the way Mr and Mrs Lancaster do business!' Laura returned firmly. 'They're straightforward and honest. If you want to buy Monk's Inn, go and speak to them openly!'

'What are you making such a fuss about? All I'm asking you to do is help me a little,' Shaun began tersely. 'Just a word here and there. It could make all the difference. I really want Monk's!' He caught both her hands urgently. 'And I thought you'd want what I want!'

Laura snatched her hands free, her heart pounding. 'I do! But you're not being fair!' she cried passionately, her eyes smarting with hot tears. 'I can't do it. I won't do it. Not even for you!'

'Laura – calm down!' Shaun exclaimed in amazement. 'There's no need to make such a fuss!'

Laura gazed at him. Despite the warmth of the room, her hands were cold. Suddenly, she didn't seem to know Shaun at all. She shivered.

'Am I really asking so much?' he persisted. 'Business is business. If you and I are–'

'No!' There was determination in Laura's quiet voice. She heard Shaun's sharp intake of breath as he half turned from her to stare into the fire. When he faced her again, he gave a conciliatory smile.

'Why don't we just agree to differ – for the time being?' he suggested mildly. 'All I ask is that you don't mention my plans to anyone until I find the right moment to talk to the Lancasters. Will you at least do that for me?'

Laura knew they'd been on the brink of having a real row. As she felt the tension ebbing, she returned Shaun's smile.

'When I want something badly, I want it now. Often I push too hard,' Shaun told her frankly, moving towards her and gently taking her hands. 'It's a problem, and I admit it. But whatever our differences, I don't want to quarrel over them.'

'Neither do I,' Laura replied softly.

'I don't want to lose you,' he murmured, kissing Laura's fingertips before slowly drawing her into his arms. 'And I don't want to waste this romantic fire-light either.'

'Thanks for holding the fort, dear!' Beattie Lancaster said, bustling into the hotel and putting down her shopping bags.

It was Laura's Saturday off – and the day of the Sandford Christmas Fayre – but she'd popped into Monk's Inn for a few hours to put up the decorations.

'Oh, it does look nice!' Beattie was admiring her handiwork. 'Have you organised the tree yet?'

Laura shook her head, folding up the step-ladder. 'I've tried ringing the nursery, but there's no reply.'

'Good!' Beattie took off her hat and coat. 'I've just met your gran and Becky in the post office. Becky was telling me you're getting your tree from Riverside Mill. I didn't even know David had pine trees out there! Since he does, I think we should get our tree from him, too...' She smiled ruefully. 'This hasn't been much of a year for Monk's or Riverside. But, hopefully, things'll improve now for David – and, with all your hard work here, perhaps we have a bright New Year ahead, too!'

Laura forced a smile she didn't feel.

It was awful, working for Mr and Mrs Lancaster, sharing their hopes and plans for the hotel's future, yet all the while knowing Shaun intended to take it over. He obviously had still not found the right moment.

The unfortunate situation was still uppermost in Laura's mind when she left the inn and crossed the green to the village hall. Becky was helping her with the hand-knit stall at the Fayre, and soon both sisters were busily arranging socks, hats, gloves and tea-cosies.

It wasn't until Laura spotted David's van pulling up outside, that she remembered.

'Becky, why did you tell Mrs Lancaster we were getting our Christmas tree from Riverside?'

'Because we are! And soon, too.' Becky's sharp eyes had glimpsed David entering the hall, his arms filled with trays of plants and flowering bulbs. She stood on tiptoe and waved enthusiastically. 'David! Over here!'

He peered over the topmost tray and

grinned broadly. Setting down the plants, he crossed the hall.

'Hello, David,' Laura said, adding needlessly, 'I see you're doing the plant stall.'

'First time I've been in charge of a stall,' he replied amiably. 'To be honest, I fancied the cakes and candies, but Mrs Almond said I looked far too lean and hungry.' David gave a resigned shrug and considered Becky's display of tea-cosies. 'Very impressive! Will you help me set out my stall later?'

The little girl nodded readily. 'Is it still all right for us to have that Christmas tree down by the stile?' she asked.

'Of course – if you put it back after Christmas!' He laughed.

Laura remembered the tree now. Late last spring, she and David had been picnicking with Becky at the edge of the small wood that skirted one of Riverside Mill's boundaries. Becky and Smokey had gone exploring, and discovered several pines growing amongst the thicket of sprawling sycamore. Trust Becky to remember David had promised she could have the tree at Christmas!

Laura recalled something else, too, with a curious mixture of sadness and regret. It was the afternoon of the Sandford Christmas Fayre that she and David had first met.

She glanced at him, chattering and laughing with Becky. It seemed a lifetime ago! So much had happened. So many changes.

'We can dig up the tree whenever you're ready, Becky,' David was saying.

'There's an afternoon when Daddy doesn't have to give any lessons, so he's taking Louise Christmas shopping in town,' Becky replied, her forehead creased into concentration. 'I think it's next week – so Laura and me will fetch the tree then.'

'Steady on!' Laura chipped in. 'Next week is awfully early. We usually leave the tree until the last minute.'

'This year's different. Louise hasn't had a proper Christmas before,' Becky answered seriously. 'Daddy wants it to be extra-special for her. He said he'll keep her out of the way in town, while we get the tree for a big surprise.

'Daddy and me only planned it last night when we were reading our story,' Becky informed her. 'We couldn't tell you, because you were out with Shaun.'

'Oh.' Laura was fussing with the fringes of a blue scarf. 'Well, that's what we'll do, then.'

'Just let me know when you're coming.' David smiled easily.

It was a raw, bleak afternoon when Laura and Becky walked Smokey over to Riverside for the Christmas tree.

David took them back to Spryglass in his van.

'Are you sure the tree will be OK in the

hall?' David queried, glancing back at the tall, bushy pine.

'Just until Dad and Louise get home,' Laura replied. 'Becky wants them to see it as soon as they open the front door.'

'She's really thrilled about it all, isn't she?' David said affectionately.

'Christmas means more to her than ever this year.' Laura smiled, showing him out. 'Dad being here ... and Louise. The whole family will be together.'

David started down the steps, and Laura followed him.

'Would you like to come for dinner tonight?' she asked tentatively. 'We'll be decorating the tree afterwards ... we'd all like you to join us.'

'You're sure?' He met her eyes levelly.

'I've been intending – wanting – to ask you for ages,' she confided uneasily. 'I never wanted you to stay away from the family, because of what happened between you and me... Please come.'

'I will. Thank you.'

As they reached the gate, Shaun Pembridge's car drew up. He parked, but didn't get out.

David glanced at his watch, going to his van. 'See you in about an hour, then?'

When the van pulled away, Shaun strode from his car.

'What's going on?' he demanded. 'I come

157

to see you – and find you asking your ex-boyfriend to dinner!'

'Oh, Shaun, don't be ridiculous!' Laura exclaimed shortly.

'Oh, so I'm supposed to like your inviting–'

'David is a family friend, coming to a family dinner. If you disapprove of that, well, I'm sorry, but I think you're being unreasonable and–'

'All right! All right! I give up!' Shaun grinned at her, holding up both hands. 'I was out of line, I apologise!'

'So you should!' She was unable to prevent herself smiling. 'Shall we stay out here in the freezing cold, or would you like to come in?'

'I would, but I can't. I'm on my way to Liverpool on business,' he replied. 'But I do want to take you out this evening.'

Laura shook her head ruefully. 'We're decorating the tree.'

'Well, when you've finished with the fairy lights, call me.' He paused. 'The Lancasters have decided to sell Monk's Inn. I want to go out tonight so we can drink a toast to the future – *our* future!'

An Unexpected Guest

James was enjoying college. He was studying hard, developing both as musician and composer. But it wasn't all work. James shared a house in Manchester with nine other students and, apart from the occasional squabble, they had a lot of fun together. He'd already made several firm friends.

Packing the last of his clothes into a suitcase, James glanced around his shoe-box of a room to make sure he hadn't forgotten anything. College was terrific, but he was looking forward to being at home for Christmas. One of the reasons for this was that the local minister had asked him to write a piece for the Christmas services.

Rehearsals at Sandford village church were progressing far better than James had dared hope, a few days later.

He was quietly whistling the melody he had composed, as he sat in his bedroom at Spryglass wrapping Becky's present.

He was going over to Riverside Mill later. There'd been an unexpected rush of pre-Christmas orders for vegetables and salad produce and David was working flat out to supply it.

He simply couldn't afford to turn business away.

So, whenever James wasn't at church, he was helping at Riverside. He glanced from the window. Sleet – again! He and David would be frozen stiff and drenched – again! But not even that prospect could dampen James' high spirits today. He'd had a letter from Charlotte.

Becky and Smokey were galloping up the stairs and along the landing.

James hurriedly stuffed her half-wrapped present into his wardrobe. He was slamming the door shut when Becky burst into the room.

'The mince-pies are ready–' she began, staring at him suspiciously. 'What are you doing?'

'Nothing!'

'You were wrapping something up!'

'I wasn't!'

But Becky had already spotted the sticky tape and ribbon on James' bed. Her inquisitive gaze swept the room.

'You were! I heard the paper rustling!'

'No, honestly…'

'It's in the wardrobe–' She darted forward.

James got there before her, and held the door shut.

'OK. Your present's in my wardrobe,' he admitted. 'But I want you to promise you won't look.'

She lowered her eyes, chewing the inside of her cheek.

'Well?'

'I promise,' she agreed reluctantly, as James bustled her out on to the landing and down to the kitchen.

'Your pies are great, Becky!' James declared, when they were sitting at the table. 'Haven't broken my teeth on the pastry or anything!'

'Your baking is lovely!' Louise smiled across at James. 'Ignore your brother – he's in love!' Becky looked at James curiously.

'What did Charlotte have to say?' Louise added. 'Or oughtn't I ask?'

'That's OK,' he replied cheerfully, unable to keep from smiling. 'Charlotte's coming on the nineteenth. I can't wait to see her!'

'Weren't you able to visit during term-time?'

'Early on, I went down to her university a couple of times. But once I got my weekend job at the supermarket...' He shrugged. 'We haven't seen each other for nearly two months. And lately, she hasn't written much. Too busy studying, I suppose. You know how ambitious she is!'

'Studying medicine is hard work. Charlotte wants to do well,' Louise reasoned sympathetically. 'So, what are your plans for your reunion?'

James beamed. 'I've got it all thought out.

Dinner at the restaurant where we went on our first date, then across the water to see "La Boheme".'

'Oh, James, that's perfect!' Louise exclaimed. The vivid opera set in Paris on a snowy Christmas Eve was one of her favourites.

'James, I don't want to offend you,' she began. 'But I was an impoverished student once myself. Opera tickets and restaurants are terribly expensive, so–'

'I understand what you're trying to say, and I'm not offended!' James came over to her chair and, putting an arm about her shoulders, bent to kiss her cheek. 'It's thoughtful of you, and I really do appreciate it. But I've saved a fair bit from my supermarket wages, so I'm OK for money.'

'If you're sure,' she returned, going with him out into the hall. 'But remember, you need only ask!'

James nodded, zipping up his waterproof jacket and considering her affectionately. What a kind and lovely woman Louise was. And what a lucky man Dad was!

'Can I come with you?' Becky was tugging his sleeve. 'I want to help, too!'

'You can't today. David and I will be out in the fields. We have to dig or cut the veg, and then weigh it and pack it into sacks ready to be sold,' James answered. 'You can come tomorrow, and work in the greenhouse packing the salad things into boxes.'

'Here, these are for you.' Becky held out a small parcel. 'Mince-pies for your tea-break. There's some for David, too.'

'Oh! Thanks!' He bent and gave her a hug. 'That reminds me – I've something else to give to David!'

James went back to the hall table and picked up the envelope which the postman had left at Spryglass earlier that morning.

David's van was just juddering to a halt outside. James turned up his collar against the icy sleet and sprinted down the path.

'Mince-pies from Becky!' He grinned, climbing into the cab. 'And an envelope from the postie. Ted said he was rushed off his feet and wasn't about to add another half-hour to his round just to deliver a Christmas card to you!'

'That's our Ted, all right!' David laughed, tearing open the envelope. 'Just brimming over with seasonal goodwill! Oh, it's from Martin Tregarth!

'We were friends when we were boys. Haven't set eyes on each other for years, but we keep in touch – sort of!' David wedged the card into the dashboard and moved off along the crescent.

'Martin's father was coxswain on the local lifeboat. Most Sundays, we'd be down at the harbour helping to swab the decks and polish the brass. We thought we were grand, I can tell you!' He laughed. 'Martin's a life-boatman in Polkerris himself now.'

'Are you going back to Cornwall for the holidays?' James enquired amiably. He was startled at the sudden grimness which darkened David's face.

'I left when I was sixteen,' he retorted brusquely. 'I've never been back. There's nothing there for me now.'

'Sorry,' James said, perplexed. 'I assumed you had family there. I didn't mean to pry.'

David sighed heavily, offering James an apologetic smile.

'You're not. It's ... oh, it's just that you think you've got the past buried then, suddenly, it's back. Haunting you all over again.' He stared intently at the curving, slush-covered road ahead.

James could no longer see his expression.

'My mother was ill for years, but she never complained,' he said at length. 'She was the gentlest woman ... yet strong, too. Much stronger than I am. Barbara and Joyce, my sisters, are a lot older than me. They looked after Mum and me and the house. Cared for my father.' He spoke the last word con-temptuously. 'Joshua Hale is a fisherman. Has his own boat. The catches were usually good, but we always seemed so poor. Barbara and Joyce always had to scrimp and save. There was never money enough for the little pleasures or comforts that might have made Mother happier.'

David paused, battling with the memories. James became increasingly uncomfortable, as though he were eavesdropping on his friend's most personal thoughts.

'I was nearly sixteen when she died,' David murmured, turning on to the rough track that led to Riverside Mill. 'Soon after, I was reading one of her favourite books. Amongst the pages was a letter from my aunt. It was obviously a reply to something Mother had written to her. I shouldn't have read it. I should have burned it straight away. But I did read it.' His voice was unusually hard, cold with fury as he recalled that day. 'Joshua Hale was deceiving my mother. She knew yet she loved him still. And forgave him.

'But I couldn't forgive him, James!' David stated bitterly. 'I'll never be able to forget the pain and unhappiness he must have caused her.'

Louise finished sewing the small, shiny wooden toggles on to the rose-pink duffel jacket she was making for Becky. She was only able to work on it when the child was at school, so she'd brought it into the dining-room to listen while James was practicing carols.

How swiftly the mood had changed! Louise's gaze wandered from her sewing to

James' violin, still across the cushion of the fireside chair where he'd left it when the telephone rang.

She heard the click of the front gate and Ken's key in the door. Quick footsteps came downstairs, and there was a brief exchange of voices out in the hall, then the front door closed with a dull bang.

'What's got into Jimmy?' Ken queried, coming into the dining-room and taking off his coat.

'Charlotte phoned.' Louise sighed sadly. 'She isn't coming home for Christmas. She's decided to go somewhere with friends from university.'

Ken raised an eyebrow. 'Left it pretty late to tell him, didn't she?' he commented. 'Hasn't he made all kinds of plans?'

'I imagine that's the last thing on his mind right now,' Louise went on. 'She didn't exactly say so, but James thinks she's met somebody else.'

'Poor Jimmy!' Ken sighed. 'He was keen on her, wasn't he?'

Louise was watching James' solitary figure down on the desolate beach, his head and shoulders hunched against the keen, off-shore wind as he walked along the water's edge.

'Talk to him, darling!' she urged, turning from the window.

'Me talk to him?' Ken echoed in consternation. 'I wouldn't know what to say.' He saw her about to protest and rushed on. 'I mean it, Louise. I could no more talk to Jimmy or Laura about – well, love and things, than fly to the moon! I'm just no good with fancy words.'

'Words don't need to be fancy, Ken!' She hugged him. 'Merely from the heart! Now – what are you going to wear for Becky's play? If it needs ironing I'll do it now.'

'Ah! I was about to get to that,' Ken said ruefully. 'The brass have unexpectedly called a staff meeting and–'

'No!' Louise cried in dismay. 'Becky's worked so hard … and she's looking forward to it very much… You've got to be there!'

'It's not as simple as that,' Ken replied shortly. 'The head of department sent a memo round making it clear he expected everyone to attend this meeting. It's obviously important.'

'More important than your daughter's first school play?' Louise demanded crossly.

Becky's struggle to overcome her reading difficulties, to conquer her shyness and actually take part in the play, had been because she wanted to please Ken and make him proud of her. The thought of her disappointment, if Ken wasn't there, made Louise angry.

'Don't you realize how much it means to Becky?'

'Of course, I do!' Ken retorted, his own temper flaring. 'Don't you think it means a lot to me, too? I'll get away as soon as I can, but if I'm not home by quarter-to, don't wait.' He scraped back his chair, snatching up his briefcase. 'You and Becky just go to the school without me!'

And that's what they had to do.

Louise had cheerfully explained that Ken would be a little late, but Becky had been subdued on the way to school. When they were about to part, she looked up at Louise trustingly.

'Daddy will come, won't he?'

Impulsively, Louise responding by doing a thing she had sworn never to do. She made Becky a promise she wasn't certain would be kept. Reassured, Becky went off to change into her costume. Louise joined the other parents in the school hall, becoming increasingly anxious as the time slipped away and Ken didn't come. She was trying to work out how to explain to Becky when the head teacher began a speech of welcome.

'Got away as quick as I could, love,' Ken murmured, slipping into the seat beside Louise just as the play began. 'Sorry I'm late!'

'You're here,' she whispered gratefully, squeezing his hand. 'And that's all that matters!'

Becky and Ken came in at the rear gate after visiting Dan. Becky ran on up to the house, but Ken hung back at the shed, where James was splitting dried-out driftwood for the fire.

Ken couldn't help admiring the way Jimmy had handled that business with Charlotte Green. He hadn't moped about, he'd kept cheerful and got on with his work. Ken was proud of him. Now he cleared his throat. 'If it gets any colder, Louise and Becky'll get their snow!'

'Wouldn't be surprised!' James agreed, blowing on his hands before swinging the axe once more.

'Where's Louise?'

'Where she always is lately.' James grinned. 'Kitchen!'

'She's fretting herself into a state over the Christmas cooking and wanting the house just so.' Ken frowned slightly. 'I expected Laura to be doing more.'

'She is working full-time now, Dad. With the Lancasters packing up, she's practically running Monk's Inn single-handed,' James said, then added scathingly, 'I expect Shaun Pembridge is delegating a lot of the reorganization to her, too!'

'Mmm, yes,' Ken conceded. 'Anyhow, that's not what I wanted to talk to you about. What are you doing about tonight? The opera, and that?'

James bent to retrieve the scattered wood. 'I'm not going.'

'That's an awful waste. I reckon you should go,' Ken said awkwardly. 'The break would do you good.'

James shook his head, stacking the kindling.

'Actually, I thought you might do me a wee favour,' Ken continued, trying again. 'Louise has hardly set foot out of the house in weeks. A trip to the opera would be a nice treat for her.'

'Yes – you're right,' James agreed readily. 'You're more than welcome to the tickets, Dad. They're good seats, and–'

'No! That's not what I had in mind. I can't abide opera! Louise dragged me along to one in Hong Kong and, believe me, once was enough. No, what I was thinking,' Ken pressed on, 'was that you could invite Louise to go with you.'

James' shy invitation surprised Louise, and delighted her, too. She suspected Ken had had a hand in it somewhere but she agreed absolutely that it would have been a shame if James had missed the opportunity to see his first opera on stage.

She dressed warmly in boots, cream trousers and a matching polo-necked jumper and went down to the dining-room. The rest of the family were gathered around the hearth toasting tea-cakes.

'You look really great!' James exclaimed, colouring and adding self-consciously, 'I mean, you always do but–'

'Thank you – and don't say another word!' She smiled, bending to kiss Ken and Becky goodbye. 'The compliment is already perfect!'

'Crossing on the ferry will be choppy,' Ken remarked, going with them to the front door. 'But I'm glad you're not taking the car. The roads'll be like glass later, if this wind freezes. Have a nice time,' he added cheerfully. 'Sooner you than me. Imagine spending three hours listening to folk howling at each other in a foreign language!'

Ken had been right about the ferry crossing being turbulent. A bone-chilling wind was whipping the river into spumy furrows, pitching the ageing vessel like a toy boat, deluging her decks with icy salt water.

Louise and James were forced to take shelter below in the saloon for the trip across the Wirral side. The journey now, on their way back, however, could not have been a greater contrast. The sea was completely calm.

'There's hardly a breath of wind now!' Louise exclaimed, as they climbed the open, metal-runged steps to the ferry's top-most deck. 'And it's almost warm, isn't it?'

'It's a lot warmer than that hall!' James laughed.

'Oh, but it was splendid, James!' Louise remarked with a contented sigh. 'The singing, the orchestra, costumes, sets – the whole production was just breathtaking! How is it that music which is sad and touching, can leave you feeling joyful and inspired?'

'I don't know.' He shrugged. 'But it happens.'

In companionable silence, they watched from the rail while the ferry began its slow, swerving course across the river.

'Look, it's snowed over in Liverpool!' Louise pointed as the white-covered roofs of the city slid into view. 'Becky will be so pleased.'

In fact, there were several patches of snow, and the temperature was still dropping steadily out at Sandford. The lanes were slippery, and it was past midnight before Louise and James got home.

'Becky and Smokey have already been playing in the snow!' James observed in a low voice. 'Look at the footprints!'

Louise laughed, slithering up the path to the porch. Ken had left the downstairs' lights on, and the old house looked warm and welcoming.

While James searched for his keys, Louise stared out across the garden.

James paused, his gaze travelling with her to the snowy shore, eerily beautiful in the hazy moonlight. It looked peculiarly poignant and lonely.

Losing Charlotte hurt. James had felt empty and pretty worthless these past days. So for him, this evening with Louise – not just dinner and the opera, but talking to her, just being with her – was like emerging from darkness into sunshine.

'Thanks for coming tonight,' he said earnestly, as she turned to face him. 'It was wonderful, really special.'

'I had a lovely time, too!' He bent to kiss Louise's cold cheek affectionately. But in that split-second, James' heart lurched, and his lips tenderly sought the warm softness of her mouth. He pulled back abruptly, breathing hard, his horrified eyes meeting hers.

'I – I'm sorry–' he stammered thickly, shocked by what he had done.

'Oh, James…' Louise murmured, sensitive to his distress, anxious that she shouldn't add to his embarrassment, or wound his pride. She gently touched his flushed cheek, searching for the right words.

Neither she nor James noticed light spilling upon them through the open front door. Or Ken standing watching from the hall.

'So – you're back at last!' Ken beamed as he drew Louise and James into Spryglass's holly-garlanded hall. 'I was about to send Smokey out with a barrel of brandy to look for you!'

'We are late – but we've had a marvellous evening.' Louise smiled, her concerned eyes

173

meeting James' for an instant before she looked again at Ken. 'You shouldn't have waited up, darling. But it's nice that you did!'

She went through to the kitchen.

'How about you, Jimmy?' Ken went on genially. 'What did you think of your first opera, then?'

'Great,' James mumbled, turning to hang up his coat.

He felt too ashamed – too guilty – to look his father in the eye.

How could he have kissed Louise like that? It seemed unbelievable.

He'd never felt more wretched in his entire life.

And what about Louise? What must she be feeling? What must she think of him now?

He liked Louise ... cared for her ... and they'd shared a special kind of companionship. But now ... in one stupid, irresponsible, childish moment, he'd ruined it all!

He was aware of his father speaking, but he wasn't really listening. All he could think of was Louise. Talking to her. Apologising. Finding a way...

Ken's words suddenly penetrated. He had opened the living-room door and gave James a push.

'In you go!' Ken grinned. 'And say hello to your visitor!'

James blundered into the comfortable room

with its glowing fire and soft lamplight. Even before the door clicked shut behind his father, the disheveled young woman who'd been sitting in the armchair was on her feet, starting towards him.

'Charlotte!' He stared at her blankly. 'What are you doing here?' She was the last person James wanted to see right now. And he was too preoccupied to be aware of the displeasure in his voice.

Charlotte stopped, took a step back, away from him. 'I wondered what sort of welcome you would give me, James,' she commented unsteadily. 'I certainly didn't expect this!'

He walked to the window, without looking at her. The heavy curtains were open, and the reflected lights of the Christmas tree made smudges of red, blue, yellow and green on the fresh snow.

'What are you doing here?' James repeated, standing with his back to her. 'Shouldn't you be on your way to Norfolk tonight?'

'I was.' There was a slight tremor in Charlotte's usually assured voice.

James turned to face her.

She shrugged.

'On the way to Norfolk, that is. When we stopped at Services, I hitched a lift to Liverpool instead.'

'That was a stupid thing to do!' James exploded.

'You imagine I'd thumb a ride if I wasn't

desperate?' she retorted, her eyes bright. 'I came to you because I believed I could rely on you. I thought you'd help me, wouldn't ask questions. But all you're doing is blaming me!'

'Charlotte–'

'Leave me alone!' She shook off the hand he'd laid on her shoulder, and bent to retrieve the suitcase beside the chair. 'If I'd wanted to be lectured, I'd have gone home to my parents!'

'You're not going anywhere tonight,' he said evenly. He'd finally gained a grip on his own composure and deliberately stood in front of the door, to stop Charlotte leaving. 'You'd better stay here.'

Surprisingly, she offered no resistance when James took the suitcase from her and set it down. All the fight and indignation seeming to have drained out of her.

'Thanks, James.' She spoke almost meekly, moving nearer but not touching him.

James gazed down into her white face, for the first time really looking at her. Charlotte wasn't the kind of girl who cried, but James realized that now tears weren't so far away.

He reached for her, and Charlotte came willingly, leaning against him, drawing comfort from his closeness.

'What is it?' he murmured thickly, his thoughts – his fears – crowding in. 'What's happened?'

She didn't speak, but James felt her clinging to him, her fingernails digging into his shoulders.

'It's all right,' he murmured soothingly, stroking her hair. 'You're safe now. I'm here...'

Another hour passed before James felt able to leave Charlotte.

She'd said little, but he'd read between the lines. An end-of-term party, everyone splitting up afterwards and going their separate ways. The offer of a ride to Norfolk with a fellow medical student...

'You're Blossoming, Laura!'

James went into the kitchen, assuming the family would all have gone to bed. He stopped abruptly when he saw Louise sitting at the fireside, the rose-pink duffel jacket she was making for Becky spread out across her lap. He'd wanted to see her, talk to her, but now he felt too ashamed, too embarrassed.

She glanced up from her sewing, and smiled at him. 'Since Becky has broken up from school, I haven't been able to finish this without her seeing it.' Louise put the work aside and got up. 'And Christmas isn't so far off now!'

'No,' James agreed uneasily.

'Laura and Becky made supper.' Louise went over to the oven. 'I've kept yours and Charlotte's warm. Would you like to take in a tray?'

'Yes, thanks. I was going to fix some coffee and something to eat.' He was hovering beside the table. 'I've told Charlotte she can stay here tonight. Is that all right?'

'Of course. Aren't her parents expecting her home?'

He shook his head. 'She's supposed to be in Norfolk. Spending the holidays with university friends. But something ... went wrong,' James finished lamely.

'I see.' Louise tactfully didn't ask for details.

'Louise – about what happened earlier,' James blurted out, unable to bear their going on as though nothing was wrong between them. 'Saying I'm sorry doesn't put it right, but–'

'James, you and I are friends.' Louise spoke very softly, coming to him and resting her hands upon his shoulders.

When James summoned the courage to meet her eyes, he saw they were solemn, but without reproach.

'When friendships are tested, they can become stronger,' she continued earnestly. 'I very much want ours to do that.'

'So do I.' James nodded gravely. 'More than anything.'

'Then I'll leave you to your supper and say good-night.'

Gently, but purposefully, she touched James' face. Everything was all right. James understood, and stooped to kiss her cheek.

'Good-night.' He returned her smile gratefully, but he still felt awful about what had happened.

'You must think only of Charlotte.' Louise had paused at the doorway. 'She's welcome to stay here as long as she wishes.'

'When she phoned to say she wasn't

coming home for Christmas, perhaps I was wrong,' James ventured slowly. 'She never actually said she wanted to break up. So maybe... Well, she has come back to me, hasn't she?'

'Yes, she has. And there will be plenty of time for you to talk later,' Louise said with a smile. 'For tonight, just have your supper and then try to get some rest. Charlotte must be exhausted, and you have to get up early to help David at Riverside.'

Charlotte was still sleeping when James left quietly a little after five-thirty next morning.

He made his way through the snowbound woods and across the ribbons of frozen river to David's market garden.

Charlotte was seldom far from his thoughts as he worked that whole day long. When the weak winter sun paled, he and David mutually agreed they'd had enough and trudged across the yard to wash and change before going into the village.

They'd arranged to run through the carol service with the organ and recorders before the choir arrived at the church for a rehearsal proper.

James was concentrating so hard on the music that he didn't notice Charlotte coming into the church. He was delighted when he glanced up and unexpectedly saw her there.

The instant the organist called a break to go over a hitch with the recorders, James set down his violin and hurried to her.

'Hi! This is nice!' Then his smile froze as he saw the suitcase at her feet.

'I'm catching the next train,' she said quietly, then quickly added before James could speak, 'I'm going to Norfolk.'

'Why?' he almost whispered, clasping her hands tightly. 'I thought you'd be here for Christmas. That we'd be together!'

'I'd planned to go to Norfolk with friends,' she said soberly. 'I don't intend to let what happened spoil my plans.'

'But won't … he … be there, too?' James persisted. 'At this house-party place?'

Charlotte's chin jutted obstinately. 'Yes. And when I see him again, I'll tell him exactly what I think of him!' She'd regained her usual confidence and self-assurance. 'It would be feeble to let someone like him ruin my Christmas. You must see that, James!'

He was too hurt to see anything much. Except the hopelessness of trying to change Charlotte's mind when she was so determined.

'At least I can see you safely on to the train,' James said simply.

'You'll miss your rehearsal,' Charlotte replied, adding more softly, 'besides, I'd rather you didn't come to see me off. It would be better if we said goodbye here.'

181

She gave him a hug, kissed him, and was gone.

James wandered out on to the church steps, watching as Charlotte walked briskly towards the railway station.

This time, it was goodbye. No doubt about that.

On Christmas morning, Louise crept downstairs long before anyone – even Becky – stirred. The sky beyond the frost-spangled windows was still dark as she worked quietly in the kitchen, meticulously following her previously-prepared list.

To everyone's delight, Dan had been discharged from hospital just two days earlier. Although he was still very much an invalid, he and Nancy were to come back to Spryglass after church and spend the day. Helen and Alex were popping in at tea-time.

'Are you winning?' Ken's voice came close to her ear. Louise jumped. She hadn't heard him coming in.

'Don't do that!' She laughed softly. 'Especially when my hands are full of trifle ingredients!'

'Hmm, looks pretty good, too!' Ken unrepentantly stole a flaked almond. 'How's the Christmas countdown going along? Everything ticked-off that should be?' He indicated the festive timetable pinned up on the cork memo board.

'Don't tease! That schedule is vital. Without it nothing would be right,' Louise admonished mildly. 'Until a few months ago, I'd little idea what a traditional Christmas was. Now I'm trying to arrange one for a dozen people. And they all know more about it than I do!'

'Look, love, if I've told you once...' Ken said patiently, pausing from setting the fire to look up at her. 'There's nothing to get yourself in a state about. It's only family, after all!'

'You're hopeless!' she returned in exasperation. 'Don't you see? It's precisely because it is our family that I'm anxious it goes well and everyone enjoys themselves!'

'What I want–' he rose, going across the kitchen to put his arms about her '–is for you to enjoy it! It's our first Christmas ... something extra special. I don't want you spending it fretting–' He broke off as he heard the almighty thumping of small feet and paws from the upper reaches of the previously silent old house. 'Brace yourself, love,' he warned. 'Here comes our own Christmas fairy!'

Seconds later, Becky charged into the kitchen wearing the rose-pink duffel jacket over her nightie. Smokey skidded around the doorway after her.

'Merry Christmas, everyone! I woke up and saw my coat at the end of my bed–' she cried breathlessly, racing into Louise's arms. 'Did you make it for me?'

'Yes.' Louise laughed, cuddling the little girl close. 'And Daddy helped!'

'I tied all the knots!' Ken grinned, holding Becky at arm's length to get a better look at the coat with its shiny wooden toggles and check-lined, quilted hood. 'You look great, Becky!'

'I woke Laura up to show her,' she said proudly. 'Then I went to show James – but he was still asleep.'

'Bet he isn't now!' Ken said drily, watching Becky as she disappeared into the pantry to fetch the container of bird-food.

'There's sponge left over from the trifle and a bag of pastry crumbs on the shelf, Becky!' Louise called, smoothing a white cloth edged with embroidered December roses over the table. 'And after you were asleep last night, David left some bruised apples...'

'I've got them.' Becky emerged with her arms full. 'I'll cut some up. I wish David was coming today. It won't be the same without him.'

'Perhaps he'll look in this evening,' Louise suggested. She and Ken had asked David to spend Christmas at Spryglass, but he'd already accepted Lyndsey McCobb's invitation to dinner at the farm.

'David's been helping out at Lyndsey's animal shelter a lot lately, hasn't he?' Ken observed casually.

'McCobb's Farm is a big place,' Louise replied, placing the breakfast dishes to warm. 'And with only Lyndsey and her brother and aunt to run it, and look after over a hundred rescued animals, there's always work needing to be done.'

'Ah, but apparently there's far more to it than work!' Ken grinned mischievously. 'By all accounts, David and Lyndsey get along very well. Not that I'm one to listen to gossip! But, when I was collecting Dan's prescription, Mrs Almond happened to mention that, in her opinion, wedding bells were in the air there!'

'Oh, no. That's not right, Daddy,' Becky commented wisely, making for the garden to feed the birds. 'Lyndsey's going to marry Mr Davenport, the vet. And David's going to marry Laura!'

'Um, thanks for sorting that out for me, Becks,' Ken said, straight-faced, winking at Louise and taking her hand as they followed Becky out into the cold, clear air.

While she filled the water bowls and scattered food, Louise and Ken strolled contentedly down the winding garden path.

'These eight months we've been married have been the best time of my whole life, Louise,' Ken said unexpectedly. Despite being so busy with all the seasonal fuss, his wife had been unusually reflective and absorbed of late. He didn't understand why. 'I've been thinking about you, though,' he went on quietly. 'You gave up your career, your father, all your friends, and even your country to marry me.

'Are you happy?' Ken asked the question hesitantly, but Louise's response was spontaneous.

'Darling – I've never been happier!' she exclaimed, astonished, yet touched, that Ken had needed to ask. 'I have never experienced so much love, or joy, as I've had from you and Becky and the family!'

Ken hugged her to him as they turned again to the house. Becky ran on ahead as she glimpsed James through the kitchen window.

'James! James! Look at my new coat!' she shouted excitedly, taking the worn stone steps in a single leap and running indoors. 'Mummy made it for me!'

'That's the first time Becky has–' Louise could say no more as her eyes filled with tears.

'It may be the first time she's said the words–' Ken took her into his arms, knowing how much this moment meant to her. 'But it's not the first time Becky has thought of you that way. She took you to her heart a long time ago!'

'Oh, Ken!' Louise held tightly on to him.

'Wouldn't it be lovely for us to have another child!'

'Steady on!' He chuckled gently. 'Don't get all misty and sentimental on me – Christmas has that effect on folk, you know!'

'It's more than Christmas. More than Becky calling me her mother,' Louise continued earnestly. 'Gradually, without realizing it in the beginning, I've been thinking more and more about a baby of our own...'

'We talked this all through before we got married,' Ken reminded her, not unkindly. 'And agreed–'

'Everything was different then,' Louise interrupted, willing him to understand. 'My world was different. I was different – I didn't feel as I do now!'

Ken sighed heavily, not wanting to upset her, today of all days. How could he tell her he was as adamantly against the notion of starting another family now, as when they'd first discussed it?

'If we had a baby, I'd be practically drawing my pension before the poor lad was a teenager,' he reasoned, frowning. 'Even if I was fifteen years younger, taking on the responsibility of another child would be foolhardy right now. If the rumours about cut-backs and job losses at work are right – well, I was last in, so I'll be first to go. And if that happens we'll be lucky to hang on to the house!' Ken couldn't disguise his anguish as he looked from Louise's wistful face to the tall, old house with its deep green woodwork and warm, cream-washed stone walls.

Although Louise didn't mention the subject again to Ken, she found herself thinking more and more often of a baby of her own. More than once, she was tempted to confide in Laura, sure that the younger woman would understand. But they had little chance to talk these days. Although Monk's Inn was now closed to the public, Laura worked late most evenings, translating Shaun's exuberant ideas and ambitious schemes into things more suitable for a small country hotel.

'You look tired!' Louise said sympathetically, fetching Laura a cup of tea as she sat at the kitchen table sorting through a sheaf of plumbing quotations.

'I am a bit!' Laura smiled, sipping the hot tea gratefully. 'It's sad to be at Monk's now that Mr and Mrs Lancaster have moved out. I'll be glad when Shaun comes back.'

'With the Lancasters gone–' Louise laughed, settling down a plate of home-baked biscuits '–your boyfriend will be your boss, too!'

'I hadn't thought of it that way before,' Laura commented. The thought unsettled her a little and she sensed Louise watching her. 'But I'm positive Shaun and I won't have any problems working together.' She gave a confident laugh.

'It must be an exciting project – all that restoration,' Louise observed conversationally. 'And demanding. I'm surprised Shaun decided to go away on holiday.'

'He wanted a few weeks in the sun that's all. Lots of folk go abroad during the winter,' Laura returned defensively. 'I'm perfectly capable of managing Monk's alone, you know!'

'I didn't mean to suggest otherwise,' Louise apologized, sitting down opposite her. 'I only meant that I was surprised at Shaun's leaving you alone.'

Laura bridled again, misconstruing Louise's words and taking her remark personally.

'As a matter of fact, he didn't want us to be parted,' she said truthfully. 'He asked me to go to Cairo with him.'

Louise frowned.

Shaun Pembridge was undeniably a handsome young man with a great deal of charm. It was easy to understand how any girl would fall for him... Especially one as guileless and trusting as Laura. She could only hope she wasn't going to be hurt.

'You're sensible to be cautious,' Louise began affectionately. 'It's sometimes better to take things slowly. I imagine some of Shaun's ideas are rather different to yours!'

To Louise's horror, Laura turned on her furiously, her cheeks burning. 'First James tries to interfere in my life, and now you! Well, you're wrong about Shaun! All of you!' Laura cried, her voice trembling. 'He loves me. And as soon as things at Monk's settle down, we'll be going away together!'

Shaun returned from Cairo looking tanned and fit and relaxed. He was in the best of moods as Laura gave him a guided tour of Monk's Inn. The old hotel was now emptied of furniture and fittings and stripped back to its original walls and floors.

'I'm wondering about changing the name,' Shaun remarked as their feet echoed on the carpetless staircase. 'Something more oldey-worldey, more attractive, than Monk's Inn.'

'I think Monk's Inn is quite attractive,' Laura replied. 'And it's certainly linked to the past. In Medieval times, there was a monastery here in Sandford, and the original building on this site was an almshouse, run by monks. After the monastery was destroyed, the almshouse became a coaching inn, then a mail-stop. Of course, over the years, it's been rebuilt and added to.'

'I'm impressed! I go away for five weeks, and when I get back, my manageress has all the renovations organized – and turned herself into a history expert! You haven't missed me at all, have you?'

'Yes, I have!' Laura laughed, manoeuvring clear of his outstretched arms as she made a space for the telephone and trays on the lobby's make-shift desk. 'And you're only fishing for compliments, anyhow!'

'True!' he admitted. 'Seriously, though. How did you find out all that stuff?'

'From Grandad. And the library. I was interested. I've also been contacting antique dealers for you to get period-style furniture and whatnot. I needed to know a little about what I was talking about.'

'You're blossoming, Laura.' Shaun gazed at her appreciatively. 'You really are – and it's beautiful for me to watch.'

Laura knew she was blushing. Quietly she bowed her head to the bundle of applications which had been received in answer to her advertisements in the local paper for kitchen and housekeeping staff. 'I'm only doing my job,' she murmured.

'And you're enjoying it, aren't you?'

'Very much.' Laura raised her face, and although her cheeks were still pink, her eyes were serious when she looked across at him. 'I never liked to be away from Spryglass and the family. Becky's always longed for a mother ... but now ... well, Louise is a terrific one. So Becky doesn't need me any more,' she finished with a self-conscious smile. 'And a whole lot of other things seem to have taken her place. All sorts of exciting prospects for the future, that I'd never dreamed were possible.'

'Feels good, doesn't it?' Shaun grinned, drawing her close to him with a contented sigh. 'Mmm, feels good... I was miserable and lonely in Cairo,' he murmured, resting his head against Laura's shoulder and kissing her neck. 'I'm not going away without you ever again. Next time, you're coming with me – and I won't listen to any arguments!'

'I won't offer any!' Laura whispered, raising her face to his.

Shaun gave a groan of pure frustration as Laura moved from his arms to answer the phone. He listened with growing impatience to the conversation.

'Laura,' he said in a low voice, coming to her side, 'put the call on hold.'

Perplexed, Laura did as she was told.

'It's Forrester's,' she began to explain. 'There's been a delay in getting that special panelling. The firm who'd agreed to supply it has–'

'I don't want Roy Forrester's excuses,' Shaun cut in tersely. 'I want that panelling! We have a schedule to keep! If one stage isn't completed on time, the next can't be and the whole job grinds to a halt!'

'It isn't Forrester's fault if–' Laura protested.

'That won't get the job done,' Shaun retorted, indicating that she continue the telephone conversation. 'Now have another go, and push him! Insist, Laura!'

Laura stared at him. They'd occasionally disagreed before, but he'd never spoken to her like this!

'It's not my way to bully folk!' she murmured steadfastly.

'Give me the phone! I'll attend to it this time.' Shaun took the receiver, holding Laura's hand for a moment longer. 'If you're going to manage a successful business, you'll have to learn to do things like this. And the sooner the better!'

Shaken, she left the lobby and went into her own office. It was just the same as it had been in the Lancasters' days, with Laura's desk and filing cabinets and her personal belongings. Although she shut the door, and concentrated hard on the order for new soft-furnishing fabrics, she could still hear Shaun's voice. He sounded arrogant and bad tempered.

Laura leaned her elbows on the desk, pressing her fingertips to her eyes. She understood Shaun's wanting Monk's Inn to be perfect. His whole future was tied up with the hotel's success.

He looked so healthy and well, at the moment, but she mustn't forget the terrible accident and how badly he'd been hurt. He must still be adjusting, coming to terms with having to rebuild his life.

'Ah – here you are!' Shaun strode into her

office with a satisfied smile. 'That's that. The panelling will arrive on time!'

'Good,' Laura replied somberly. 'But did you have to be–'

'Yes, I did! But I'm sorry I was sharp with you.' He came around and sat on the corner of her desk, obviously still pleased with the outcome of his conversation. 'One of the reasons I love you is because you're so warm and gentle.' He tilted Laura's chin, raising her face so he could kiss her mouth. 'But there are going to be occasions when you'll have to be tough.'

He kissed her again and got to his feet. 'Oh – and I want you to contact your ex-boy-friend.' Shaun laughed at Laura's surprised expression. 'There'll be lots of odd jobs needing done and, according to the church-warden and several others, David Hale works hard. And he'll come cheaply. No doubt he'll jump at the chance of some work.'

Laura sensed David's reluctance when she telephoned him at the mill later that day. Later, he came to her office at Monk's Inn.

'These are always lean months. Orders have slowed to a trickle,' David replied frankly, in response to Laura's concerned inquiry. 'The weather isn't helping – it's holding back the planting. As for the other plans I had for Riverside – well, I haven't the money now. But, you're busy. I mustn't keep you.' He changed the subject briskly, draining his coffee cup and getting to his feet. 'Thanks for the offer of work, Laura. I'll take it – and be glad of it!'

From the very first day there was a wary hostility between David and Shaun. On far too many occasions, Laura saw David swallowing his pride, silently accepting Shaun's criticism and getting on with his work.

Then early one morning, the simmering antagonism between the two men erupted into an ugly scene. Laura had never seen David so angry.

'You hired me to do a job – and I'm doing it!' His dark eyes glinted with resentment. 'But work like this can't be rushed. If it's to be done properly, it takes time!'

'And the more time you take,' Shaun cut in accusingly, 'the more money you–'

'Stop it! Both of you!' Laura rushed into the dining-room to find them standing in front of the fireplace, which David had been painstakingly rebuilding. 'I could hear your voices outside!'

They both turned to look at her.

'David would never cheat anyone, Shaun! You should know that!'

'Keep out of this, Laura,' he retorted warningly, glancing at her in annoyance. 'This isn't anything to do with you. Go to your office!'

Laura gasped in shock and David made an

almost imperceptible move towards her. She met his eyes briefly, before turning on her heel and leaving them alone. She walked quickly across the lobby towards her office, then hesitated at the open doorway. With a shake of her head she went on past it and out into the cobbled yard.

Standing in the welcome silence, Laura stared through the archway and along the winding lane. She was tempted to go straight home – and never come back. No, that wouldn't be right. She sat down dejectedly on the edge of the old horse-trough which Mrs Lancaster had planted with flowers and heather.

How long she sat there, alone with her troubled thoughts, she wasn't sure.

At last, Shaun came quietly across the yard and sat beside her.

'I was worried. You weren't in your office.' He took her hand gently.

Laura didn't respond. Or look at him.

'That argument … don't let it upset you. It's just–'

'Business?' Laura demanded bitterly, glaring at him. 'Don't say it – because it doesn't matter! I can't go on this way. All we've done recently is disagree and argue about business,' she went on unsteadily, annoyed at the tears that were threatening to spill over. 'What's happening to us? What's happened to being in love?'

'Stress is getting to us both,' Shaun murmured, taking a handkerchief from his pocket and dabbing her wet eyes. 'It hurts me to see you this way. And I blame myself for being too absorbed to realize how unhappy you've been. We need time alone. Away from Sandford,' he concluded softly.

'We've talked about going away, but we've never got around to it. Maybe we should go now, because once Monk's reopens, there'll be no chance of our taking a break together for months.'

'That's true,' Laura faltered. 'But I don't know. I'm just not sure.'

'We owe it to ourselves. To each other,' Shaun persisted, stroking her face tenderly with his fingertips. 'What do you say?'

Laura gazed into his eyes. Then she nodded.

'I'll get on to Miles Weaver and make a few arrangements,' he said quietly. 'With luck, we'll be on our way to Stratford-upon-Avon by this time tomorrow!'

'So soon?' Laura asked as he rose from her side. 'Can we just leave the inn like that?'

'There isn't anything more important to me than your happiness,' Shaun answered simply. 'It may not always seem so, but you have to believe it's true.'

She smiled at him, warmed by the ray of hope. Perhaps they could recapture the joy and wonder of being in love.

Typically of Shaun, his idea became reality in less than fifteen minutes. He insisted Laura take the rest of the day off to pack and get ready. With an easier mind and lighter spirits, Laura dealt with the letters on her desk before starting home.

Second Thoughts

Laura was at the edge of the village when a police car from the local station drew alongside.

'Laura!' John Hammond rolled down the window and leaned out. 'I'm looking for David. Someone said he was working at Monk's Inn. Is he there now?'

'Yes.' Laura was alarmed at his grave urgency. 'What's wrong?'

'I'm afraid I've some very bad news for David...'

'Mr Hammond!' Laura began, cold with foreboding. 'Can I come with you?'

The police officer opened the passenger door and she got into the car.

'Can you tell me what's happened?' she blurted out as they drove into the village.

John Hammond glanced at her, consideringly. 'I don't see why not.' He sighed heavily. 'It seems a pal of David's is coxswain of the Polkerris lifeboat—'

'Martin Tregarth?' Laura interrupted anxiously. David rarely spoke of his past, but he'd mentioned his boyhood friend to her. 'Has something happened to him?'

'No. It's David's father, Joshua Hale,' the

officer related bleakly. 'His fishing boat is missing. The lifeboat's been out since dawn. Helicopter's out searching, too, but...'

'Poor David...' Laura whispered.

'Apparently, David's sisters tried phoning him at Riverside Mill...'

'He's been working at Monk's Inn since early this morning,' Laura told him.

'Ay. Anyhow, Martin Tregarth radioed a message through to Sandford Coastguard and they got on to me.'

They were approaching Monk's Inn. Laura turned to him.

'Let me tell him,' she implored. She couldn't bear the idea of David hearing the news in cold, official language. 'You know how close we used to be. I'd like to be the one to...'

'All right,' John Hammond agreed quietly. 'But are you sure, Laura?'

She nodded unhappily, then got out of the car and ran into Monk's Inn.

David appeared to take the news calmly, but Laura watched the colour drain from his face. She led him into her office and he sat down as she warmed the pot for tea.

David hardly said a word, but she recognized the turmoil of conflicting emotions in his eyes. How could she ease his pain?

'I haven't seen my father since I was sixteen,' David murmured at length. 'Some-times I've wondered if I was wrong to let it go on, but I could never bring myself to make the first move. Not after what he did.' He sighed, his eyes meeting hers only fleetingly. 'I suppose I thought there was plenty of time ... that one day... But now it's too late!'

'Don't say that!' Laura cried emphatically. 'They're still searching. Your father could be found! There's still hope!'

'Yes, of course there is,' he returned softly, looking up at her as she brought the tea. 'But, remember, I know the sea round Polkerris. At this time of year it can be treacherous – particularly for a small boat.' He shook his head slowly. 'I'm afraid there's little chance of my father being found alive. I'd better call Barbara and Joyce, my sisters. This will be terrible for them.' He pushed his hand through his hair in a distracted gesture. 'Then I must go down to Cornwall.'

'Phone your sisters from here. And I'll come to Cornwall with you!' Laura said impulsively, thoughts of her holiday with Shaun banished from her mind. 'You can't go by yourself, David!'

'Thank you, Laura.' His voice was quiet, and very gentle, and he moved as though to touch her face. Then he drew back. 'You're a good friend. You'll never know how grateful I am that you were here today.' He reached out and gripped both her hands, smiling up into her eyes.

The fleeting glimpse of their old closeness tore at Laura's heart.

'And thank you for offering to come to Cornwall – but it's one journey I have to make alone,' David finished gently.

Laura took a quick, unsteady breath, her hands still resting in his. She was regretfully conscious of the once-familiar tenderness of David's touch. She withdrew her hands, turning away from him with an effort. Choking down a rush of tears, she managed to speak.

'You'll be wanting to telephone your sisters. I'll leave you in private.'

Sleep eluded Laura that night. When she got up, there was still no news from Cornwall. Later, when she returned from walking Smokey along the beach, she heard her father speaking sombrely into the telephone. She hurried through into the hall just as he was replacing the receiver.

'The search for Joshua Hale has been called off,' Ken said simply. 'David says he'll be staying with his sisters until the end of the week. There'll be arrangements to be–' He broke off at the sound of Becky's footsteps on the landing.

The little girl loved David like another big brother. Why upset her by telling her what had happened? At least, not unless she herself asked.

'So, Laura,' he went on brightly. 'Got your bag packed and ready for the off, are you?'

'Yes,' Laura answered reluctantly, mindful that her young sister was within hearing. 'But how can I possibly go away?'

'What reason is there for you not to go?' he countered practically. 'We're all thinking about David, but there's nothing we can do. You missing your holiday won't help – and David would be the first to tell you so!'

Later, when Shaun arrived at Spryglass, he found Laura sad and subdued. He'd already heard about David Hale's father – word had gone around Sandford like wildfire. Neighbourly concern it might be, but Shaun regarded the local preoccupation with minding other people's business as one of the more irritating aspects of village life.

Nonetheless, he appreciated Laura's distress, and was sympathetic and understanding. Gradually he coaxed her into conversation as the miles to Stratford-upon-Avon slipped away.

Finally, Shaun's efforts were rewarded. He sensed Laura beginning to relax, responding with the warm smile he'd come to cherish.

Laura hadn't been to Stratford before and, although there'd be plenty of time for sight-seeing after lunch, Shaun couldn't resist taking her to see Anne Hathaway's cottage. Half hidden by thick green hedges, with its tiny leaded windows peeping out from beneath thick folds of undulating nut-brown thatch, the cottage glowed in the early sunshine.

'It's beautiful!' she murmured, entranced.

'So are you,' he returned simply, taking her into his arms and kissing her.

Holding hands, they continued the last few miles to the Hearts Of Oak, the secluded sixteenth-century tavern where they were to spend their holiday.

'I especially asked Miles to give us this room,' Shaun began, unlatching the low door and standing aside for Laura to enter.

She paused at the doorway to admire the oak-beamed bedroom with its creamy-washed stone walls, open hearth and antique furnishings.

'It's got the best views in the whole place,' he went on, slipping his arm about Laura's waist, and leading her to the bowed windows. 'Look, darling. A lake! With swans—' He broke off, sensing Laura's sudden tension.

'It's all right, isn't it?' Shaun's question was uncharacteristically tentative. 'The room, I mean?'

'Y-yes,' Laura faltered uncertainly, not meeting his eyes. Instead she concentrated on the sweeping expanse of shining, willow-fringed water with its gliding, snowy-white swans. 'You're right, the view's lovely.'

'You know that isn't what I meant.'

Laura's gaze met Shaun's for the briefest instant. 'It's just ... well, I hadn't expected–' she began awkwardly, avoiding his eyes. 'You didn't say anything, and I...'

He drew her to him, holding her gently. 'I took a few things for granted, didn't I?' he murmured ruefully. 'But I don't want to rush you. If you're not happy with this, I can easily make other arrangements. Whatever you want–' He inclined his head so he could look at her properly. 'It's all right.'

'Oh, Shaun!' she murmured, his gentle solicitude provoking her emotional response.

After lunch, they spent the afternoon strolling hand in hand along the banks of the River Avon. Then they explored the market town of Stratford.

'Tomorrow, we can follow the valley down into the Cotswolds,' Shaun was saying when they lingered at the lake to watch the setting sun spill paintbox colours into the still, shimmering water. 'Go on to Bath, if you like.' He pulled her near and kissed her as they turned their backs on the lake and started up towards the tavern. 'We'll decide over dinner.'

Laura had enjoyed their day, but now she had fallen silent, her thoughts troubled.

'Shaun – wait!' She caught his arm as they made to enter the tavern. 'This isn't right! I shouldn't be here with you!'

He turned to face her, reaching for her, murmuring reassurance.

Laura wasn't listening. She couldn't hear anything but the thumping of her own heart. Her throat was dry, and it was all she could do to frame the words.

'I thought – but I was wrong. Now I know I–' she stammered wretchedly. 'I don't love you, Shaun. I'm sorry! I'm so desperately sorry... For all of this,' she finished in a small voice.

'Not wanting to be with me is bad enough,' Shaun said savagely, staring past her to the darkening lake. 'Apologising makes it even worse!'

'I only meant I was sorry for hurting you!' she murmured in confusion.

'It's David Hale, isn't it?' Shaun demanded angrily, his hands gripping her shoulders so hard Laura had to face him.

'No! It isn't!' she cried honestly. 'He and I are friends – nothing more!'

'Friends?' he challenged bitterly. 'Perhaps you believe that – but I don't. You're in love with David Hale... You've never stopped loving him!'

The spring morning was dark and chilly. Ken got up first to light the fire in the kitchen ready for when Louise came down to prepare the family's breakfast. In the grey half-light of dawn, he watched small blue

206

flames flicker over the salty driftwood.

They'd been married for almost a year, and Ken had been planning a celebration. He wanted to take Louise on holiday and she'd always shown so much interest in Scotland. It was years since he'd last been there, and he had no desire to go back to the poor pit village where he'd spent his boyhood, but he had been looking forward to touring the Highlands.

Now, he thought, perhaps it was fortunate he hadn't booked or made any proper arrangements. Plans like that would have to wait. He'd have to keep an eye on every penny. Months of rumour, about staff cut-backs and departmental closures, had become hard fact during last evening's meeting. Ken knew he might not have a job much longer.

Hearing Louise opening the front door to get the milk, he got up and put the kettle on.

Louise never ate breakfast herself, but when Becky and Laura's was ready and keeping hot on the stove, she brought her coffee around to Ken's side of the table.

'Why didn't you wake me when you got home last night?' she asked.

'It was awfully late. Hours of talk – but nothing was actually said!'

'So have they decided to give your department the funds it needs to continue?' Louise's voice was concerned.

'You've got to be joking!' he retorted derisively. 'No – they've appointed a committee to make a report! Funds will be allocated according to their recommendations. Which means we'll all be kept waiting until the end of next month!' Ken finished in annoyance.

Louise laid her head against his shoulder in a wordless, sympathetic gesture. She knew that, behind Ken's anger and impatience, was a deep-rooted fear of unemployment. She was scared, too.

'Darling, if you lost your job, will you go back to sea?' She fought to keep the anxiety out of her voice.

'The last thing I want to do is leave you and the family,' Ken answered thickly. 'But it wouldn't be easy for me to get another teaching job. Going back to sea might be the only way out.'

'There is another way,' Louise ventured quietly. 'Me! My designing and dressmaking! There's a shop to let in the village. Next to the newsagents'. It has everything I'd need and the rent's reasonable.'

'If a shop is what you want, then I'll not stand in your way,' he responded stiffly. 'As to the rest – well, if you're interested in my opinion, I don't like the idea!'

'You're just being selfish! You're considering only yourself – not the family or me!' she cried. 'I loved my work and my shop. I miss the challenge and the stimulation – the sense of achieving something in my life!'

'I'd no idea you were so dissatisfied with our marriage,' he said coldly. 'You've a home and a family – I thought that was what every woman wanted. It was always enough for Jeanette. She was never restless–'

He was interrupted by Laura and Becky coming down for breakfast. After that, there was neither the opportunity nor the time for further discussion.

During the weeks that followed, Ken was irritable and short tempered. Louise became increasingly unsettled. Restlessly, she spring-cleaned Spryglass from loft to cellars.

Then she made new quilt-covers and, with Laura's help, painted and papered the girls' bedroom.

'Want to beak for a cuppa?' Laura asked, noticing Louise running a hand wearily across her forehead as they fitted wallpaper around an awkwardly-sloping corner of the attic room. 'You look shattered!'

'I'm a bit tired, that's all. I'm fine. Really.' Louise smiled. 'Besides, you've been working at the hotel all day.'

'Oh, I enjoy this!' Laura replied enthusiastically, straightening up and admiring the room. 'Anyway, although business is better, now we're fully staffed, my job isn't so hectic.'

'It can't have been easy for you to stay on,' Louise commented mildly.

'I didn't think it would work, at first,' Laura confessed, speaking for the first time about her break-up with Shaun. 'I offered my resignation, but Shaun refused to accept it. He knew how much I enjoy my job, and told me I should stay. It was such a generous thing to do – I'll never call him selfish again. And it was awful for both of us at first.

'But I'm glad we persevered, because it is becoming easier,' she finished self-consciously.

Louise was less than convinced of the nobility of Shaun's motives. Laura was a conscientious hard-working girl – an asset to any enterprise.

'I'm glad for you,' she said genuinely. 'You've worked so hard. You deserve every success!'

'Thank you,' Laura smiled. 'You haven't been inside Monk's Inn since we re-opened, have you? I'd enjoy showing you around. If you'd like to come, that is. Perhaps we could have lunch together afterwards...'

'Oh, that would be lovely!' Louise beamed, pleasure bringing a touch of colour to her pale features. 'I'd love to come!'

They arranged to meet at Monk's Inn at eleven o'clock on Wednesday.

Louise didn't arrive on time. When she still hadn't shown up half an hour later, Laura was concerned.

She telephoned Spryglass, but didn't get a

reply. Her father had the car, so Louise would be walking into the village.

Laura left her office and went outside to see if she could see Louise coming along the lane.

There was no sign of her. Laura was turning to go back inside when she saw Louise sitting hunched and alone on the bench beneath the oak tree on the green.

'Louise!' she called, springing across the grass. 'I've been waiting–' She broke off as she drew near. Louise's face was wet with tears. 'Whatever's the matter?'

'I'm going to have a baby... I didn't even suspect I was pregnant. Isn't that silly?'

Louise stared fixedly at the grass with its patches of tiny white daisies.

'But it's wonderful!' Laura was perplexed. 'Aren't you pleased?'

'Oh! If only you knew how I've longed for a baby.' Louise paused, raising anguished eyes. 'But Ken and I agreed. He doesn't want another child.'

'Riverside's starting to look good again, David.' James gave the fields full of growing vegetables a backward glance as he and David wheeled barrows towards the barn. 'Grandad was showing me the greenhouses earlier. You're growing more indoors than ever!'

'Thanks to Dan!' David responded with a

smile. 'We're partners now.'

Since Dan's illness, David had taken care of all the heavy work on his allotment. Dan came out to Riverside three days each week to work in the greenhouses.

'Provided we're not flooded again this summer, and if there are no other unforeseen expenses, I should just about break even.' He paused. 'I'm not afraid of hard work. And I never expected running my own place to be easy,' he went on, going to the barn's open doorway and standing on the threshold. 'But lately I've been wondering if it's worth it.'

He raised a hand in response to Dan's wave and he and James crossed to the mill. Becky and Smokey were sitting like statues amongst the bluebells and hares-tail, watching the brown and yellow ducklings bobbing after their mother in the river.

'Tea-break, Becky!' David called. She tiptoed away from the bank.

'I wasn't expecting visitors today – especially not a young lady,' David told Becky as they all went indoors. 'Your granddad and I are used to roughing it at tea-break – isn't that right, Dan?'

'Oh, ay,' he agreed gravely. 'Tin mug of cold water with a few bits of soil in, that suits us champion!'

'But I'll find something a bit tastier for you, Becky.' David went into the sparse, antiquated kitchen, with Becky following him. 'Let's see what there is in the cupboard. We'll have whatever's there!'

Becky shook her head indulgently. Rolling up her sleeves, she began to wash her hands at the sink. 'You've been working hard all day,' she said seriously. 'Go and sit down with the others. I'll make our tea.'

'I know another girl who used to say that to me.' David laughed quietly, handing Becky a towel. 'Funny – she looked a bit like you, too!'

Becky laughed with him, before bundling him from the kitchen and opening the bread bin.

'You're not serious about giving up, are you?' James persisted as they settled in the living-room.

'Oh, I suppose not,' David replied, tilting his ladder-backed chair and rocking meditatively. 'Riverside's what I always wanted. And I do like being my own boss... On the other hand, the idea of starting at nine, finishing at five, and collecting a nice, regular wage-packet is awfully tempting!'

'That's not everything it's cracked up to be,' James said with feeling. 'Ask Dad!'

'Ken told me he might lose his job.' David frowned. 'Report's due the week after next, isn't it?'

'Yes. I know how I felt when I was waiting to hear if I'd got a place at music college,'

James recalled grimly. 'Goodness knows what Dad's going through.'

'Ay, Nancy and I were saying much the same on Sunday when we got home from having tea with you,' Dan put in thoughtfully. 'We don't want to interfere, but we'd like to help.' He looked at James. 'Do you think there's anything we can do?'

'I don't know, Grandad.' James considered, pausing reflectively. 'I don't think so. I've only been home a few days, but I have the feeling there's something else bothering Louise. Besides Dad's job, I mean. She just isn't herself.'

'Louise is going to have a baby,' Becky announced matter-of-factly. She walked across the room, taking small, careful steps as she balanced the tray of tea and sandwiches. 'I heard her and Laura talking. Daddy doesn't know. It's a secret.' She looked sternly at each of them. 'I'm knitting bootees for the baby. And that's a secret, too!'

They'd hardly started their tea when the telephone rang. James was sitting nearest, so he got up to answer it. The caller spoke rapidly and without pause. James made several attempts to interrupt. When he did, he asked the distraught woman to wait and turned to the others, his face suddenly grave.

'David, it's one of your sisters. She's very upset. Your father's b–' James checked, aware that Becky was listening and re-phrased what he had been about to say. 'They've found him, David.'

David was grateful that James went with him to Polkerris, for Joshua Hale's funeral. After the service, he and James and Martin Tregarth walked slowly from the church down into the middle of the small fishing town.

David and James had booked in at The Mermaid And Castle.

'Maybe this isn't the time to mention it, Davey,' Martin began, 'but Minnow wasn't damaged much.'

David nodded. Joshua Hale's boat had been recovered weeks before.

'Me and a couple of lads have done a bit of work on her, so she's perfectly sea-worthy now,' Martin went on. 'What I'm getting around to saying, is that you could do a lot worse than coming back to Polkerris and taking over your dad's fishing–' He was interrupted by the shrill bleep of his pager. 'That's a shout! I got to go!' Martin was already running along the steep, twisting street. 'See you both later–'

'Take care!' David called after him, but Martin had already turned the corner toward the lifeboat station.

David watched him go, his gaze gradually drifting across the harbour to the calm sea. 'I'm taking Minnow out for a blow, James,' he murmured thoughtfully. 'Want to come?' Within half an hour, they'd left the harbour behind and were out on the open sea.

David was strangely pleased at how familiar Minnow felt. He'd forgotten that a boat became more than timber and metal once she touched water, suddenly taking on the vitality and spirit of a living thing.

'You look the part!' James commented with a smile, standing beside him in the wheelhouse and admiring his friend's confident handling of the vessel.

'This is what my father wanted me to do,' David returned simply. 'He expected me to take over the boat and the fishing after he'd gone– There's the cottage I grew up in!' He pointed back to the crooked rows of houses and scattered white-washed cottages. 'The one at the end of the harbour road. My sisters still live there, of course.'

James nodded. He'd seen for himself how strained the relations between David and his two older sisters were.

'They don't know about your father, do they?' he said evenly. 'What you found out about him? When you left home?'

'I've never told anybody except you.' David pushed open the wheelhouse window so the fresh salt air rushed in. 'Barbara and Joyce worshipped my father. I couldn't hurt them by telling them he'd been deceiving our mother for all those years. So I just left without giving any reason. My sisters didn't understand – and didn't approve. They thought I was letting down my father, and my family. As the only son, I had a duty to stay and take over the fishing.'

'Is that what you'll do now?'

'I don't know. I've thought about leaving Sandford,' David admitted frankly. 'But coming back to Cornwall? It'd never entered my head until today. But, with things so uncertain at the mill, I'll have to give it some serious consideration. What I decide now could change the rest of my life.'

'Let's Go Home!'

Unable to bear the thought of David coming back from his father's funeral to a cold and empty house, Laura had borrowed the spare key from Dan and had come to light the fire and prepare a meal.

David wasn't due for another half-hour.

'I saw you through the window. You shouldn't have...' David began quietly, glancing around the warm, welcoming room. 'But thank you.' He smiled, closing the door and taking off his coat.

'I wasn't... You're early,' she faltered at last, struggling to get a grip on her feelings. 'How are you? And your sisters?'

'I'm OK,' he replied, but a concerned frown creased his forehead. 'Barbara and Joyce have taken it awfully hard. Barbara, particularly. She's not been well, what with the shock and...' He sighed heavily. 'She's pretty poorly. They've been understanding at the chandler's where she works, but it looks as though she'll have to give up her job.'

'Oh, that's a pity,' Laura returned sadly. 'I'm so sorry, David.'

'Yes,' he agreed. 'And something unexpected came up just before we left. It was Martin who–' David hesitated, looking down into her face.

'It'll keep. I'll tell you another time.' He shrugged dismissively. 'That wouldn't be one of your casseroles I can smell cooking?'

'It'll be another twenty minutes or so.' Laura forced a bright smile, picking up her bag and jacket. 'But everything else is ready. There's a fruit pie–'

'Won't you stay?' David asked quickly, realizing she was about to hurry away. 'Please?'

Laura paused. Perhaps he needed somebody to talk to? She nodded.

'Oh, David,' she murmured sympathetically. 'Was it awful? Polkerris, I mean?'

'No. Not really,' he answered frankly. 'I can't explain it, but when James and I took my father's boat out, I suddenly didn't feel bitter any more. All the old hurts were gone. And I was remembering Dad the way he used to be, when I was a boy. I thought the world of him then!' He smiled sadly. 'Respected and admired him. Wanted to grow up to be just like him.

'On summer nights, Dad, Martin and I used to go sailing. We'd sleep on deck under the stars. If only I could see him, talk to him, just once more! Tell him I–' David's voice cracked, and he swiftly averted his eyes, swallowing convulsively.

'David...' Laura whispered his name, reaching out awkwardly to pat his hand. With all her heart she longed to wrap her arms about him and comfort him. 'It's all right,' she continued gently. 'It's as it should be, David.'

Supper was strained. There was none of the easy conversation and comfortable silences of their old days together. Laura guessed David was as relieved as she was when the meal was eventually over.

'I wish you'd let me see you home,' David said as she picked up her coat. 'I don't like letting you go alone.'

'I'd rather,' Laura insisted, more sharply than she'd intended. 'Really.'

'OK.' He gave a resigned sigh. She obviously didn't want to stay at Riverside – or with him – a minute longer than necessary. He walked with her to the door, standing behind her to help her on with her jacket. His hands rested lightly on her shoulders.

Laura's breath caught. If she walked away now, without saying anything ... would she be making the same mistake again?

'David – I love you!' She spoke very softly, without turning to look at him. When he didn't respond, she wondered desperately if he'd heard her. Gently he brought her around to face him.

'Then marry me, Laura,' he said urgently, drawing her close against him.

Laura had popped into the newsagent's in the village during her lunch-hour to choose a greetings card. She was reading the verse on one with a beautiful flower picture when she became aware of somebody sidling alongside her.

'If I tell you I love you–' the low voice was close to her ear '–will you let me walk you back to work?'

'David?' she inquired innocently, still reading. 'Is that you?'

'Who else were you expecting?' he demanded, bending to kiss her.

'Not here!' Laura hissed, giving him a push. 'Mrs Almond is over by the magazines!'

'You're right. I should be ashamed of myself,' he agreed soberly, but his eyes were twinkling. 'What are you buying?'

'Birthday card for Gran,' she answered.

When they'd left the shop, David slipped his arm around Laura's waist. 'Are you sure you wouldn't like to go away somewhere after our wedding?' he asked. 'I know we don't have much money, but Riverside is doing reasonably well now.'

'Oh, David, it isn't because of the money – really it isn't!' Laura glanced quickly around the lane before reaching up to kiss him. 'The only honeymoon I want is being together in our own home!'

'OK.' David gave in amiably, kissing Laura slowly, despite her protests that the postman was cycling by. 'But if you should change your mind...'

Laura nodded, her cheeks pink. As they approached Monk's Inn, David paused, taking both her hands into his. 'You know how I feel about our working together at Riverside after we're married,' he began seriously. 'But it's a big decision for you. Why don't you think it over a while longer?'

'I don't need to,' she replied simply. 'I'm going to give Shaun my notice.'

'You expect me to accept this?' Shaun retorted later that afternoon, tossing aside Laura's letter of resignation. 'You expect me to be all noble and civilized, to just stand by and watch you throw your whole future away?'

'I'll stay on until you find a replacement.'

'You think that's what I'm concerned about? A manageress for this place?' Shaun's voice was scathing. 'You're making the biggest mistake of your life. The only reason I've said nothing before now, is because I hoped you'd come to your senses!'

'Please – don't!' Laura implored miserably. 'If you go on like this, you'll hurt us both!'

'Hurt! You don't know the meaning of the word!' he exploded brutally. 'Try watching the person you love marrying somebody else. Then you'll know hurt!'

Spryglass's garden was golden with billowing daffodils, and the late spring sunshine was warm enough for Louise to take her sewing outdoors. She was letting down the hem of Becky's best dress, so she could wear it at the weekend when Ken arrived back from Southampton.

He'd been away on field-trips with his students from the college before, but Louise had never missed him quite as much as she'd done this time. Part of her wanted to share the wonder of these early weeks of her pregnancy with him. Another part was anxious about how he'd react when she told him about the baby.

Louise's concentration strayed from her needlework. Whatever the consequences, she'd be grateful when the college announced its decision on Friday. Ken would be home again the following day.

If only he'd be pleased they were to have a baby... If only he didn't lose his job... If only he wasn't compelled to rejoin the Merchant Navy... Her needle and thread darted swiftly through the fabric. So many if onlys!

When the hem was finished, she went inside to press the dress. As she was setting up the ironing board, the telephone rang.

'Ken – I was just thinking about you!' she exclaimed in delight. He usually didn't call until tea-time, when Becky was in from school. 'Oh, it's marvellous to hear your voice!'

'Steady on!' He sounded pleased. 'I never realised I could be as lonely as I've been this past week. All I've done is think...' Ken paused, a shade awkwardly. 'Anyway, since I was in the area I've been catching up with a few old friends. From my Navy days. If I do get the push, there's a decent chance I can get a job down here in Southampton.'

Louise tensed, her fingers closing tightly about the telephone. Ken was going back to sea! He'd be away for months at a time. She'd be without him.

'Are you still there?'

'Yes,' she murmured somberly. 'I'm listening.'

'I'll explain properly when I see you,' he went on hurriedly. 'But basically, it's short European routes. I'd be home three days out of every fortnight. Far from perfect, I know, but it would tide me over until I can get another shore job.'

'I'd miss you terribly, but it's far better than I dared hope!'

'And it would be just temporary,' he insisted, breaking off. 'I'll have to go. Somebody else wants to use the phone. See you on Saturday.'

Very late on Friday night Ken silently let himself into Spryglass. The porch light was on and the front door unbolted, so he guessed Laura was still at Monk's Inn. He left his suitcase in the hall and went upstairs. Louise wasn't in their room, so he started up to the attic.

The door was ajar. He could see Louise sitting on the corner of Becky's bed, her arm around the little girl's shoulders. They were both fast asleep, the book they'd been reading lying open upon the quilt.

Seeing his wife with Becky like this... Somehow he knew he was right. He'd missed a great deal during his years at sea. Laura and James growing up, all Becky's younger days. He hadn't even been at home when his children were born; he'd first seen their faces in photographs. But marriage to Louise had changed everything.

Tiptoeing into the room, he closed the storybook and bent to touch his lips to Louise's forehead. She stirred, opening sleepy eyes.

'Ken!' she exclaimed softly, trying to ease away from Becky without waking her. 'What are you–'

Ken beamed and took her hand. He led his wife out on to the landing before taking her into his arms.

'Soon as the lecture finished, I started driving home,' he whispered. 'I didn't want to spend another night away from you.'

To her horror and dismay, Louise started

to cry. And couldn't stop. She fell against Ken, holding on to him with all her strength.

'It's all right, love... Just let it come,' he soothed, resting his cheek against the smoothness of her hair. 'You're having a baby, aren't you?'

Louise raised wet eyes to him and tried to speak. When she found she couldn't she nodded incoherently.

'I wanted to tell you,' she sobbed at last. 'When you came home. Tomorrow...'

'If you like, I can go away again and–' Ken began cheerfully, trying to make her smile. Then he read the uncertainty in her eyes and understood.

'I'm delighted about the baby!' Ken's voice was gentle, but his arms held her all the more securely. 'You believe that, don't you?'

She stared up at him, a glimmer of joy appearing in her dark eyes.

'I want to believe it,' she whispered hesitantly.

'Believe it,' he said simply, dabbing her face with his handkerchief. 'Oh, I know I said I didn't want to start another family ... but I feel differently about it now. During the past few days, I've sort of got used to the idea, you see. There's nothing like spending his evenings all alone in a hotel room for giving a man time to think. And mostly I thought about you. The notion you might be pregnant sort of crept up on me.' He took Louise's face in his hands and kissed her. 'I guessed a bit – and hoped a lot!'

'Why didn't you say something?' she asked in surprise.

'Over the phone? No way!' Ken shook his head. 'I wanted us to be together. I wanted to be able to see you ... hold you.' He paused uneasily. 'I'm no good at saying things like this, but I couldn't be happier or prouder than I am tonight!'

'Darling, you don't have to–' Louise faltered as new and powerful emotions engulfed her. Her smile was now mingled with more tears.

'Hey, don't start that again!' Ken protested, putting his arm about her shoulders. 'I haven't got another dry hanky! Come on, let's go downstairs and I'll make cocoa,' he said with a tender smile.

'Want a refill?' he inquired a little later, when Louise was curled up beside him on the couch.

She shook her head, nestling closer. 'Just you.'

'You've already got me!' he joked. 'And that reminds me – I've got some news, too. Not as good as yours, but I think you might be pleased! You know that seagoing job I told you about? I won't be applying after all.' Ken paused, smiling and watching Louise's face.

'Just before I left Southampton, the principal got in touch with the report's recommendations. There'll be voluntary early retirements and streamlining, but no department closures or job losses. My job's safe!'

'Oh, thank goodness!' She hugged him fiercely. 'You deserve it. You work incredibly hard, and you're a fine teacher!'

'Steady on!' He laughed, fending her off. 'You'll spill my cocoa!' He fished into the pocket of his shirt, and withdrew a small box tied with ribbon. 'This is for you.'

Louise untied the ribbon and opened it. She gasped as the light gleamed upon a silver brooch, set with a single, richly-glowing amethyst.

'Oh, Ken!' she whispered. 'It's beautiful!'

'It's a thistle. They grow in Scotland,' he commented gravely. 'Thought you might fancy a wee holiday, touring the Highlands and seeing the real thing–'

'Daddy!' Becky and Smokey exploded into the quietness. The little girl clambered up on to Ken's knees and the dog tried to do the same. 'You're back! I've missed you! Are we really going to Scotland?'

'Who's got big ears, then? Yes, we're really going to Scotland.' He grinned at Louise and winked. 'All four of us!'

'Five!' Becky said quickly.

'Five?' Ken repeated, looking anxious. 'Expecting twins, are we, Becky?'

'No.' She shook her head solemnly. 'I meant Smokey. He can come with us, can't he?'

'Ay, why not!' Ken laughed, tousling Becky's fair curls. 'We'll all go – right after Laura's wedding.'

Spryglass was in chaos. James had been awake all night practicing the piece he'd written for the simple service Laura and David had chosen at the village church. Ken was up a stepladder decorating the hall with the garlands of fresh flowers Dan had brought from his allotment at dawn.

Nancy, Helen and Louise were organizing the kitchen, because Laura and David, instead of a fussy reception, had asked for a quiet family gathering. Sadly, Barbara Hale's illness had prevented David's sisters from attending, but Martin Tregarth had travelled up from Polkerris to be best man.

'Louise!' Laura raced downstairs and burst into the kitchen, her face flushed. 'I can't find my shoes. Will you come and help me, please?'

'Of course.' Louise dried her hands, taking a quick look around the kitchen. Everything looked more or less ready. And the three-tiered cake Nancy had baked and iced was safely out of harm's way in the pantry.

'Becky! It's time you were getting dressed!' she called, hurrying through the hall. 'You, too, Ken!'

'I'll worry about that when I've got these flowers right.' He leaned back a fraction on the ladder, squinting up at his handiwork. 'Are they straight?'

But Louise was already upstairs and following Laura into the attic bedroom. Carefully she removed the ivory-coloured dress from its protective coverings. She'd hoped to design and make the wedding dress herself, but she'd also understood Laura's wish to wear the gown which had belonged to her great-grandmother and had been worn by Nancy and her own mother, too. The princess-seamed front bodice was laid-on with delicate Victoria lace and the full, fluted skirt fell to a gracefully shaped hem.

Laura was taller than the earlier brides, and Louise had taken great pride and pleasure in making the alterations.

'It's an exquisite dress!' She smiled. 'You look lovely. I wish you and David every happiness and blessing in your marriage.'

'Thank you!' Laura turned around, shyly giving Louise a little hug. 'If we're as happy as you and Dad–'

'Is anybody up there?' Ken's exasperated voice drifted up from the foot of the stairs. 'If we don't get to the church soon, David will think you're not coming!'

Laura was full of plans to grow herbs, cut flowers and a greater variety of soft fruits at Riverside. And she was looking forward to planting wallflowers in the sheltered, sunny corners around the house. The fragrant plants were David's favourite. As she watched David collecting the post, she was imagining their dark curling leaves and velvety flowers…

'Card from the family!' He smiled, holding it up.

'Mmm, Loch Katrine!' Laura exclaimed appreciatively, slipping her arm through David's. 'What's your letter?'

'It's from Boscombe's – the solicitors in Polkerris.'

Laura watched his expression become solemn as he read the contents.

'Not bad news?' She gave his arm a squeeze.

'No. Nothing like that. It's about Dad…' David murmured, re-reading the letter as they wandered down to the seat beneath the willows. 'We assumed he'd never made a will, but he had. Martin was doing some routine maintenance on the boat, and found it – and all Dad's personal papers, and a coin collection – squirreled away behind the paneling in the wheelhouse.

'My father didn't trust banks any more than he trusted lawyers!' David concluded with a small smile, passing the letter to

Laura. 'Dad's left the cottage to Barbara and Joyce, but he wanted me to have his collection. I didn't even know he was interested in old coins!'

'Oh, David...' Laura reached up and put her arms about him, hugging him. 'I know you've been unhappy, wondering how your father felt about you in his later years...' She faltered, trying to find the right words. 'It's sad – I suppose legacies always are – but at the same time, it proves that your father never stopped thinking of you, or–'

'I know what you mean.' He smiled ruefully, gently threading his fingers into the softness of Laura's hair and drawing her closer. 'Apparently, Dad collected those coins over fifty-odd years,' he continued at length. 'According to Boscombe, the collection will fetch a sizeable sum.'

David glanced up at her quickly. Was she already aware of what was running through his mind?'

'We made our plans long before this came up,' Laura reminded him gently. 'You and I – we have everything. Our health and strength ... and each other. We're already rich! But your sisters... Barbara's had to give up her job, and Joyce can only work part-time... You're thinking of making over the legacy to them, aren't you?' she murmured.

'I can't deny it. Dad meant well, but he couldn't see how things would turn out for my sisters,' David said quietly, gazing at her. 'I'd be uncomfortable if I kept even a penny of that money.'

'I know you would,' Laura traced the line of his jaw with her fingertip. 'And I'm proud of you because of it.'

Laura was working on Harvest Festival Sunday. She went into Monk's Inn several hours early so she could get away in good time for church. She and David were meeting the family and Gran and Grandad, and all going to the service together. As summer became autumn, the inn's guest rooms were no longer fully occupied. But business was still brisk, especially for dinner and weekend lunch bookings.

So far, Shaun hadn't mentioned his plans for the Christmas and New Year season. In fact, he'd been delegating more and more responsibility to Laura, frequently spending days away without getting in touch. Going through the lobby, Laura saw a light under Shaun's door. It wasn't like him to be in his office at this hour on a Sunday morning! She knocked and looked in.

'Shaun, I'll need your signature – Mr Weaver!' Laura broke off, recognizing the man sitting there. They'd met once before, in Stratford-upon-Avon, where Miles Weaver owned the Hearts of Oak hotel.

'It's Laura, isn't it? Hello, again!' He

smiled warmly and shook her hand. 'I'm just getting my bearings. Sorting out the important stuff, such as where the coffee and biscuits are kept! I was hoping for a chat, but I didn't expect you in this early! Won't you take a seat?' he said pleasantly.

'I'll be here for the next three days, but I'll try not to get in the way!' he went on briskly. 'I'm not making any changes yet, so it's business as usual!'

'Mr Weaver, I'm sorry, but I don't quite understand...'

Miles Weaver looked at her perplexed face, and raised an eyebrow. 'My apologies. I naturally assumed you'd be aware of the situation,' he began evenly. 'Shaun has sold Monk's Inn. I'm the new owner.'

'I see.'

'I want you to stay on, of course,' he added quickly.

'Thank you, but I resigned a while ago,' Laura explained quietly. 'I've only been staying on until Shaun found another manageress.'

'Ah, I understand,' Miles commented, recalling Shaun's fondness for Laura. 'Well, let me make a few phone calls. I'm sure we can sort something out.'

Laura went to her own office at the rear of the inn. The instant she pushed open the door, she saw the posy of flowers on her desk.

Apricot carnations and tiny, creamy-white rosebuds.

The flowers Shaun had always given her. They'd cared – loved – each other once.

Wherever Shaun was, whatever he might do in his life, Laura hoped he would find happiness.

Sadly she held the posy in her hands. This was surely the loneliest way for them to part...

Laura finished off the work she had pending and cleared her desk. Miles Weaver couldn't have been nicer or more helpful, releasing her immediately.

Leaving Monk's Inn for the last time, Laura paused in the lobby, looking round affectionately.

Then she went outside and crossed to the green.

The family were already there, chatting to other folk from the village. David and Becky were shuffling through crinkled, golden leaves, deep in discussion about Grandad's wood-carving skills.

Laura fell into step beside them, slipping her hand into David's. Becky was wide-eyed, bubbling with excitement.

'Grandad's finished making–' she began, breaking off as she spotted the posy. 'They're pretty!'

'Yes, aren't they?' Laura smiled, offering

the flowers to her young sister. 'Would you like to put them with ours, for the Harvest Festival?'

Becky nodded, adding them to her own bunch of colourful chrysanthemums and dahlias.

'Grandad's finished carving the cradle!' she continued enthusiastically. 'And Gran's made a frilly wee pillow and bumper. Louise said it's lovely, and Daddy said we're all ready for the Big Day!'

Rose was born during the winter's first frost-spangled night. On the afternoon Ken and Becky set off to bring her and Louise home to Spryglass, the old house's gardens were white with a powdering of fresh-fallen snow.

Laura filled the dining-room with bowls of freesias from Riverside's greenhouses, then left David lighting the fire while she prepared a meal for the family. Returning to the cosy room a little later, Laura went to draw the curtains. She paused briefly to gaze beyond the garden to the shore and the distant grey thread of ocean. There was scarcely a breath of wind, and everywhere was very still.

'It's starting to snow again.' She half-turned to smile at David, and he came to her side.

'The first time I ever saw you, you had

snowflakes in your hair!' he said, moving his hands slowly up and down her arms. 'Have you given any more thought to that honeymoon you haven't let me take you on yet?'

'Mmm, as a matter of fact, I have!' Laura replied with a quiet laugh. 'I'd like to go to Cornwall. Meet your sisters and see Polkerris. Explore all the places you've told me about.'

'Sounds wonderful to me!' he responded, his mouth finding the sensitive hollow behind Laura's ear.

They were still kissing when the garden gate creaked open. Louise and Becky came in, followed more slowly by Ken, who was carefully carrying the baby.

Becky broke away, racing up the snowy path and bursting in at Spryglass's front door.

'Laura! David! We're here! We've brought Rose!'

Shortly afterwards, Laura and David left Spryglass.

'Didn't you want to stay for tea?' David inquired in some surprise.

Laura shook her head contentedly.

She paused at the gate to return a cheery wave to the family before they went back indoors.

'It's their day, David.'

He nodded, taking her hand and starting along the lane, but Laura pulled free, sprinting away from him.

'The tide's coming in!' she called over her shoulder, running across the snow-brushed shore. 'Let's go home along the beach!'

David caught up with her, swirling her into his arms. 'Say it again!' he demanded, his eyes shining. 'I like hearing you say that!'

'Let's go home, David!' Laura laughed breathlessly, standing on tiptoe to kiss him. 'Let's go home...'

The publishers hope that this book has given you enjoyable reading. Large Print Books are especially designed to be as easy to see and hold as possible. If you wish a complete list of our books please ask at your local library or write directly to:

Dales Large Print Books
Magna House, Long Preston,
Skipton, North Yorkshire.
BD23 4ND

This Large Print Book, for people
who cannot read normal print,
is published under the auspices of

THE ULVERSCROFT FOUNDATION